Lovin' Danger

Mata Hari Series, #4

A Novella

by

Jo-Ann Carson

Copyright

Lovin' Danger is a work of fiction. Names, characters, places and incidents are the products of the author's imagination or are used fictitiously. Any resemblance to actual events, locales, or persons, living or dead, is entirely coincidental.

Praise for Lovin' Danger

"...pulse-pounding thrills, spicy sex and unforgettable characters....

~ Mimi Barbour, New York Times Best-selling author

Praise for the Mata Hari Series

"...Ms. Carson writes an action-packed suspense with incredible pacing and well-developed characters that readers will thoroughly enjoy. Sadie is a strong and sassy heroine and is well matched with Sebastian; the chemistry between them is off the charts and the adventures they experience while traveling Europe to complete her mission are described in great detail and with fantastic imagery. Readers will not want to put this book [Covert Danger] down and will be eagerly awaiting the next installment in the series."

Molly Daniels **(InD'tale Magazine, June 2015)** 5 stars, 5 steam pots for steaminess and a crowned heart for excellence

The Mata Hari Series:

#1 - Covert Danger

#2 - Born of Magic

#3 – Ancient Danger

CHAPTER ONE

New York City
Wednesday April 1st

Sadie woke gasping for air, her body covered in sweat, her nerves trembling. Damn dreams. They always haunted her before something really bad happened. She glanced at her radio clock, 8a.m., too early to face the day. Settling her head back into her soft pillow she reminded herself premonitions were useless superstitions. That's when she heard a knocking on her front door. Grabbing her Glock 36 resting on the bedside table, she listened for more sounds. Her senses sharpened as the world slid into slow motion. More knocking, harder this time. She shook her hair out of her face as she moved towards the sound.

Releasing the safety on her gun, she looked

through the security lens. A soon as Sadie recognized her visitor, the tension in her body eased and she drew a long, deep breath. *Not an assassin this time.* She put the safety back on the gun and placed it on the entrance table, then released three deadbolt locks and cracked the door open. After taking a good look around, she opened it wider to greet her friend.

Wearing a pink, sweat suit and smelling of peppermints, her neighbour Beatrice pushed past Sadie and strode into the room. She had the awkward gait of a woman determined to be three steps ahead of her body, but held back by an arthritic hip. A fluffy labradoodle puppy, Casanova, followed at her heels. His tail wagged like an out-of-control metronome. Bee took a quick look around the apartment, then turned and fixed her eyes on Sadie.

Sadie closed the door and stood in front of the table where she had placed her gun. Beatrice knew she lived a dangerous life, but didn't need to know how dangerous.

Beatrice looked her up and down as if Sadie hid secrets in her belly button. "Took you long enough to answer the damn door."

Sadie shrugged and stared back at her. Curlers with bristles held the woman's blond hair in neat rows on the right side of her head, while her hair fell loose on the other side. It didn't take a Sherlock to know the woman had rushed over. "Do you know what time it is?"

"I need a favor," Beatrice began.

So they talked and talked. The banter flowed back and forth like a tennis rally for five minutes and then stopped at the net. They stood facing each other in an uncomfortable silence.

Beatrice looked over her pearl rimmed glasses, perched near the bottom of her long nose. "Cheekbones, ya only live once." Her tobacco-worn voice made her words sound prophetic and sometimes Sadie thought they actually were, but not today.

Sadie had things to do. The spook part of her wanted to rest after spending a late night sleuthing around a gala event at the Met Opera. The model part of her wanted to soak her aching feet, currently holding at a nine on her ten-point, blister scale. Standing for hours on stilettos never got easy. And the girly-girl part of her wanted to phone her lover, Sebastian, and have a good, long chat. Well, maybe a dirty-chat.

She sighed at that thought. There was so much for her do in her hectic life and not enough time to savor the best parts. And on top of that, not being able to succeed at her new goal—to find balance in her life—frustrated the heck out of her. No one wrote, "How to Find Balance," articles for spies. No one espoused instant remedies for the chaos created by what life threw at spooks. She had to figure it out on her own.

Beatrice raised a brow.

Sadie's eyes slid down to the ground. Casanova, a chocolate labradoodle they shared, sat between them, his leather lead in his mouth. He looked from one woman to the other with hope in his gorgeous eyes. Drool foamed at the right edge of his mouth. As if he understood they neared a decision, he let out one long, pathetic groan.

"Okay you got me," Sadie said. Cassy had clinched the deal.

***

Four hours later, Sadie looked around Bryant Park in mid-town Manhattan checking out the scene. It's natural for people to enjoy spring, a time of fertility, energy and growth; but this one, coming on the heels of a wicked winter, created an unprecedented thawing-out excitement in the city that hung in the air like a delicious contagion, infecting everyone with joie de vivre. A hundred people flowed through the small park. Groups gathered sipping coffee and chatting as if they hadn't seen each other for a decade. Old men played chess with young men. Lovers held hands. A lone musician played a Stradivarius violin. Laughing children skipped along the path. And they all smiled as they shared in the warmth of the sun. Sadie breathed it all in. Maybe an afternoon in the park would be help her with her balance goal.

Lovers held hands. A lone musician played a fiolin. Laughing children skipped along the paths. And they all smiled as they shared in the warmth of the sun. Sadie breathed it all in. Maybe an afternoon in the park would be good for her.

As if he heard her thoughts, Cassy nudged her

thigh. The heat of the sun sizzled on Sadie's skin. The day seemed perfect. Almost too perfect. That creepy-cold-as-ice feeling tip toed up her spine. Was she imagining it? Had to be. *Premonitions aren't real.*

She sat with Beatrice and her two friends at a square, card table. Sadie's eyes swept her surroundings, on guard for the unexpected. But who would bother her in a park?

"Now get this straight, Cheekbones. It ain't poker we're playin' here. Don't go all cut- throat on us."

Sadie screwed up her face. Beatrice liked to call her, "Cheekbones," because she made good money pouting in front of cameras. The world thought she was beautiful, but when Sadie looked at herself in the mirror, all she saw was the skinny girl from the wrong side of Seattle. If others wanted to give her attention for her looks, that suited her fine. It made a great cover for her work with the CIA. Sadie shrugged. "Just tell me the rules."

"What? You never played bridge before?" The lady to her left, called Mabel, paled. Her face contorted, as if she had gas.

"It can't be that hard," Sadie said widening her eyes and forcing her mouth to remain straight.

"I ya yi." Jane, the lady to her right, slapped the table with her hand. "A virgin."

Beatrice shook her head. "Ah, don't worry about it. This one's smart as a whip." But her hand trembled, as she shuffled the cards.

"So we have partners?" Sadie knew how to play bridge well enough for an afternoon with the ladies, but playing Beatrice was much more fun. "Do we have a secret handshake or something?"

Beatrice gave her the evil eye. "Pick up your damn cards and sort them in suits." She exhaled a lungful of cigarette smoke. "Talkin' about partners. Where's that handsome giant of yours."

"In Amsterdam." Sadie sighed. "He has an important business meeting."

"Sheesh, you two. You need to spend more time together. Make it real, you know."

Real? Her relationship with Sebastian couldn't be more real. But she got Beatrice's point. Being a long-distance couple had its challenges.

"You two, shut up already," said Jane. "Are we here to play cards or talk men?"

Sadie smiled. "So when do I get to give my bad cards away?"

Bee grumbled and pointed two fingers at her own eyes and then at Sadie's, the classic, "I'm watching you" look.

Sadie laughed. "Okay, I'll be serious."

Beatrice grunted. "You need to figure out how many. . ." Her words faded.

People in the park started murmuring all at once. Some stood and pointed to the east. Sadie couldn't see anything, but she could hear a buzzing sound, like a large mosquito. Scratch that, like a horde of mosquitoes. The buzz grew louder and louder.

Then she saw it. "Ladies, take cover."

As she stood up, she pulled her gun from her purse and aimed it at the approaching drone, just in case. It floated in space surveying the area with a camera. About two feet in diameter, it looked like an electronic, hunter spider with a big body in the middle and many arms stretching out, each equipped with propellers. Below the body hung a lens the size of an eyeball and below that a square package. That package could be dangerous.

People started screaming and ran to get away from the specter. The drone made wide circles above the people.

The rotating eye faced Sadie and stopped. Oh no! It stopped. The grumble of the engine increased and headed straight toward her. The whooping of the tiny propellers and the buzz of the engine grew louder and more distinct.

Mabel and Jane ran for the library which adjoined the park, but not Beatrice. Standing at Sadie's side, she raised her purse, ready to take a good swing at it. "I didn't tell you to bring a friend." Cassy barked.

"Call 911," Sadie said. "Take Cassy and run." The drone, now ten yards away, closed in.

Should she shoot? It might explode. Sadie started jogging backwards. The drone followed. If she could get into the library and close the door she'd be safe, but then others might not be. Was it on a timer or remotely controlled? She couldn't risk taking her eyes off of it to look for a control man on the ground. He could be in the crowd or miles away.

A security guard in uniform came out of the library. Thank God. He started moving people back. The police would be on their way. But not in time.

How could she draw the drone away from the crowds? Where in Manhattan are there no crowds? Five yards and closing in. If she threw a coat on top of it, would it be blinded? Maybe, but a blind drone could still be dangerous. What if she threw a rock at it? What if... Time was running out. And Beatrice hadn't moved from her side. Cassy kept barking and leaped into the air.

Sweat beaded above Sadie's upper lip. *Ah hell.* She steadied both her hands on her gun and shot above the package, hoping to kill the engine. " Boom!"

CHAPTER TWO

Leonidas Krykos IV followed what the press called "the Manhattan drone attack" and he called "a fucking disaster" on the big-screen TV in his hotel room. His own, on-the-spot view through the lens of the camera died the moment the drone exploded into a million pieces.

Sadie Stewart. What a bitch. He clenched his jaw.

Police and fire sirens blared. People who initially ran away from the drone, now wandered back to check out the scene. City police had cordoned off the area where his drone, which he named "Avenger," exploded. Scores of men in uniforms searched the area for clues. They would find bits and pieces of his machine, but they wouldn't find him. Hopefully.

Leon studied the TV screen, hoping to spot Sadie, but the crowds of spectators grew and pressed in around the tape. He doubted she had stuck around, or returned. Why would she take that risk? No, she was probably somewhere far away and safe. Damn it.

The drone should have worked. He scratched the stubble on his chin and grunted. He had followed her and her friend to the park, then went back to his room and readied the drone. But allnd his efforts were for nothing.

What a fucking mess. He'd spent a week creating the drone from scratch so that no one could trace it back to him. Avenger worked perfectly and she had been the best solution. Efficient and deadly. But she fucked up. Or he did.

He poured himself a cognac with a shaking hand and gulped it down.

The woman had pulled a gun. A gun! Why would the bitch have a gun? And why would she be a crack shot? They said she was a beautiful model, not a commando. There was more to this woman than he'd been told.

He unclenched his fists and began pacing the room. How could this have happened? He had followed her for two weeks, watched her go to shoots, dine with other models and lift weights in the gym. He'd followed her on her runs in Central Park. There

had been nothing in her behavior to suggest she was a fucking sharp shooter.

He poured another glass.

What had he missed? Should he do more surveillance? Maybe meet her in person? That would take time. Time he didn't have. His father wanted him to kill her and get out. "Fast and invisible," were the words he used over and over again. The KOTL wanted her dead—ASAP. His father would be muttering about now, muttering about him and his incompetence.

Would they send someone to kill him? It was possible. They might consider him a potential leak. They didn't like regular people to know about their secrets or their mission. But his father would stall them, perhaps long enough for Leon to finish what he had set out to do.

Would the American cops find him? Cold sweat
trickled down the back of his neck. Doubtful. Sadie
Stewart had hit the engine dead-on causing it to
explode. The drone would be in at least a hundred
charred pieces.

Besides, he'd been careful to purchase the parts
in different cities under different names and used
rubber gloves to put it together in a pristine lab. He had
covered his trail, done all the right stuff. But he hadn't
got the girl. He excelled and detail and he had carefully
planned every step of the kill. But it all went wrong.
Damn that woman.

A red ribbon with the text, "Breaking News,"
slithered across the bottom of the TV screen, catching
his eye. He turned up the volume. A well-shaped, blond
announcer with fish lips painted bright red stood in
front of the tape. "I'm here in Bryant Park, at the scene
of the drone incident. Twenty minutes ago a drone
descended on the peaceful grassy area behind me. Yes,
a drone." She motioned to the area with her hand. The
camera shifted to show the grassy meadow in the
middle of the park. "It flew low," she continued, "so low

many thought it would shoot them all. People started running away. Except for one woman. She pulled a gun out and shot it."

The gun-toters of America would eat this story up.

A picture of a drone similar to his model, Avenger, flashed on the screen. But Avenger had been better made than the machine they showed. "Observers say that it looked like this, a standard carrier-pigeon drone used to carry small objects. One man said he saw a camera and a shooting mechanism on it." The picture went off the screen and the announcer reappeared.

The sound of the crowd murmuring around her produced a low hum in the background. "Another eye-witness told me," she continued, "the drone was honing in on the shooter. Why? No one knows. The drone blew up when the woman shot it and the police are picking up the pieces. The shooter disappeared."

The camera panned the cordoned-off area again. "Police are collecting eye witness reports on the incident to learn more. They want to identify the shooter. At the moment they have more questions than answers." The drone facsimile went up again. "If you know anything about this drone, or the shooter, please call... A list of phone numbers and a website were put on the screen and she read them out.

Leon groaned. There's nothing like having one of the largest cities in the world looking for you. Eight and a half million people. Fuck. How could a simple kill go so wrong?

Bile rose in his throat. He needed his inheritance. He deserved his inheritance. He couldn't let that red-headed bitch get in his way. He poured a third glass. Damn, he had had a bad feeling about this so-called mission from the moment he'd been given it.

He'd walked into it blindfolded. No one blindfolds an assassin. Idiots. Didn't they want him to succeed? He had to find out more about the target. There had to be a way to kill her. Achilles had a weakness. Sadie had to have hers.

On the TV screen the announcer talked to an older woman dressed in a sweat suit. "I understand you were here when it happened."

"Oh yeah, I was here. I told the cops

everything."

"What can you tell us about the shooter?"

"A real looker. . . with a big dog. A good shot too. She saved us."

"Thank you," the announcer said. She turned away from the woman and looked directly at the camera, filling the screen with her image. "If anyone out there has a photo or video of the incident, please contact the police. . ." The numbers rolled again.

A woman with a dog. He'd been beat by a woman with a... dog.

CHAPTER THREE

Amsterdam

Sebastian Wilde loved everything

about his life except *this*. The pile of paper in front of
him had grown to two feet, and every single sheet
needed his attention. He picked up the top one,
scrunched it into a tight ball and launched it into the air.
Watching it arc then drop into the wastepaper basket
on the other side of his office gave him almost as much
pleasure as a bottle of beer. *Aced it.*

His life was near perfect. He loved Sadie Stewart
more than he thought a guy like him could. He loved his
zany Tante Zen who raised him and the Van der Valk
clan who adopted him into their extended family. His
business, dealing modern art, rocked. Helping his friend

Seamus at Interpol nail assholes who traded looted art was cool too. But what he didn't like, didn't like with a passion, was paperwork. Another projectile flew into the air, but this one missed the target. *Godverdomme.*

It didn't matter how many assistants he hired, the damn pile of paper grew on his desk like cultured, zombie babies in a Petri dish. By the time he dealt with one invoice, twenty more piled up. Did the sheets mate when he wasn't looking? His eyes crossed from reading and signing invoices, letters, memos and legal documents. Should he set the whole pile on fire? He rubbing the bridge of his nose. That wouldn't work. His assistant would have copies.

He groaned at the mountain he had to climb. There were no avoiding it. He needed to clear his desk, and get the big meeting over so he could be with Sadie.

In two hours that meeting with the infamous Walter Easterbrook, a British dot.com guy who bought art for investment and prestige would take place in Seb's office. It was probably the biggest deal in his art-dealing career so far. His assistant had summoned him back to Amsterdam just for this event.

A deal with this guy meant big bucks and a bigger reputation. Sebastian hadn't wanted to leave Sadie, but meeting Walter was not only an honor, it was an event that could cement his business, the kind of event he would tell his grandchildren about. Grandchildren? Where the hell did that thought come from?

Leaning back in his chair, he looked out the window on the second floor of his canal house. The busyness of the morning bicycle commuters made him smile. Working at home had its advantages. People flowed up and down both sides of the still canal. A mother heading for the local school balanced her son and daughter on her bike, one in front on the handlebars and one in back on a carrier above the wheel. A businessman in a suit peddled his bike with his mobile phone attached to one ear. An older lady cruised on her bike with an enormous bundle of pink tulips in the front basket. Tourists took pictures of the comings and goings with mobile phones and iPads. One carried an old-fashioned camera with a long lens. Seb could spend all day watching people in his hood.

He'd left the window opened at the bottom to let the smell of baking bread from the family bakery down the street drifted in. It made him feel peaceful. He loved Amsterdam. There was no other place in the world like it. It was home.

As he studied the dark water of the canal, which looked still and reflective, a sense of foreboding ran through his mind as if it chased a conscious thought and then settled in his heart. He shook his head. Damn, he hated getting prescient feelings. Mostly because they were right.

What could go wrong? His life was good. What could possibly go wrong?

Looking at his desk he winced. Yah, the details of business were a drag, but that wouldn't give him this uneasiness, this deep-down, gut-wrenching, nerve-rattling uneasiness. He twisted his neck to ease the tension building in his muscles. His mobile rang. The screen said: Sadie.

Please, God, let it not be her. In one dramatic sweep of his arm, he shoved his paperwork off his desk. The sheets flew into the air and billowed down to the floor.

"*Mijn liefje.*"

"Seb...astian." She was panting.

"What's wrong?"

"Some asshole just tried to take me out with a...a drone."

"A drone? Like... in the air..."

"If I get my hands on the guy who controlled it."

Seb growled. It would be nothing like if he got his hands on him. Heat rushed to his face and he noticed he was standing. "You hurt?" His voice cracked.

"No. Just mad. . . Really mad."

"Mad's good. Where are you?"

"Heading home. I just. . ."

"Yeah, I know."

"I should have called Cole first. But. . ."

Cole? His blood cooled instantly as if a ton of ice chips had entered his bloodstream. Jeremiah fucking Cole was her CIA handler. The farther he could keep Sadie from him the better. "Fuck him. Where did it happen? Are you safe?" Words gushed out of his mouth.

"It happened in Bryant Park. I'm safe for now."

She filled him in on the details, as he walked out of his office and climbed up the stairs to his private apartment, what he now considered *their* private apartment. Time to pack.

"Where are you now?" he asked.

"I just got home. I need to call Cole. I'll call you back later."

Seb pulled his suitcase out of the cupboard. "Sadie."

"I'm okay. I just. . . I just wanted to hear your voice. Really, I'm okay."

He shook his head. "How's. . . your body?" He knew she'd know what he meant. Was she in shock? Had the adrenalin rush come to an end? Was she scared? There were so many things he wanted to know. He would only have to look at her for ten seconds to tell these things, but instead all he had was her voice over a mobile phone connection. Fuck. He wanted to hold her in his arms.

"Sebastian." Her voice, low and husky, raked his senses. "I'm fine."

Oh shit. When a woman says she's fine, you're

hooped. And Sadie would never admit being anything less than fine. Maybe he should try a different tact. "Mijn liefje."

She laughed at the tone of his voice, knowing exactly what he had on his mind. "You've got to be kidding."

"Do you know what I'd do to you, if I was there with you right now?"

"Tell me later." She clicked off.

****

An hour later Sadie phoned back. Sebastian had packed, cancelled his big event with Mr. dot-com, and made reservations on the next flight heading for New York. He'd be with her in a matter of hours and then he'd be able to see just how "fine" she was. His need to be with her came over him faster than a category five hurricane and with the same ferocity. Nothing mattered more than Sadie. The awareness crystalized in every cell of his body.

"Mijn liefje," he said trying to put all his emotions into the two words. That was impossible. He needed to be with her.

"Hi, honey. Sorry it took so long for me to call you back. I..."

"You alone?"

"Uh, yeah."

"You okay."

"Yeah." She hesitated. "Ooh yeah."

He leaned back in his chair smiling. "You know what I'd do to you if I were there?"

She swallowed. "Tell me."

"I'd pick you up in my arms and carry you over to the sofa. I'd lay you gently down." He paused to let the image sink in. "Then I'd do a thorough job of checking you over."

"You want to play doctor?" The lusty rasp in her voice sent his libido into hyper-drive.

"Shhhh, good patients listen."

Sadie groaned. "Not sure I can do this. I don't do docile."

"I'm not asking for comatose," he said," just... let me get started. You are the injured one, after all."

"Doctor, I've been hurt." Her voice didn't sound hurt. It sounded as provocative as all hell. Sweat trickled down the back of his neck. If only he could touch her. "My hair is loose and disheveled," she continued." My clothes are torn. I'm barely covered. My lips are swollen. . ."

"Sadie, you're killing me."

"I have an owie here. I'm pointing to my…"

"If only I could touch you." His normal voice broke through their fantasy. To hell with game playing.

"Sebastian."

"I hate being so far away from you."

"I'm all right. Honestly, I'm fine."

That fine word again. "Sadie, I don't know what I'd do if anything happened to you."

"Stud-man, you're seriously killing the mood. Come on, Sebastian, tell me what you would do if you were here."

He laughed. Only Sadie could turn a serious conversation to sex in a heartbeat. "Well," he said in a deep voice. "I need to examine your body for bruises. The owie spot will have to wait until I get there." He sighed at that thought for both of them.

She whimpered.

Hmmm. Sadie had never been a whimpering woman. She was more like a commanding, Amazon-warrior kind of lover. She'd take, ravage, scratch and scream, but never whimper. Maybe she felt like whimpering today. Maybe. Hell, was she into this fantasy, or was she just humoring him, so he would stop worrying?

"Miss Sadie, are you sure you want me to do this?"

"Doctor, I need you to do this."

"Uh-huh. Okay. I'm touching your torn blouse, considering what I should do with it."

"Oooh."

"Stroking my hands down your arms as I look over your body."

"You have such big hands, Doctor." Her breathing increased.

"Your skin feels warm and soft and inviting. I'm trying to be professional, but I'm so aroused I want to spread your legs apart and take you, hard and fast, to end the desire burning inside me. But I'm not telling you this. Slowly I run my hands over your curves. Your beautiful curves. 'Checking for broken bones,' I say."

"Am I allowed to do anything?"

"Close your eyes. Try to relax. Let Dr. Wilde give you a thorough examination."

"Mmmm. My eyes are closed."

"I continue to run my hands over your body, feeling it warm to my touch."

"Doctor…"

"As my fingers trace your breasts your breath hitches with pleasure, and my cock jerks.

"'No broken bones,' I say, 'but I'll look some more, just in case.'"

"Yes, Doctor. I want you… to be sure."

He let silence still their conversation for a moment.

"Are we alone?" she asked.

"Uh no. The two ambulance attendants, a man and a woman, are standing on the other side of the curtain, waiting to find out if they need to take you to a bigger hospital. The man is looking though the gap in the curtain, which is about an inch wide."

"He's watching us?"

"His eyes are focused on you."

Sadie sighed.

"I glare at the man who watches and then my hands return to your ripped blouse. Slowly I undo the top button, letting my fingers touch the soft skin on your breast as I do so."

"Mmmm."

"I open the second button. I'm so hot for you. I just want to rip it off. But I force myself to slow down. I open a third."

"I can feel your manly hands rough against my sensitive skin. My lower belly aches for you. I ache for you. I try to control my breathing. I try to pretend that I'm not affected by your touch, which scorches me with red-hot fucking desire."

Seb groaned. "Carefully I open your blouse, exposing two round, firm breasts partially covered by a white lace bra. My heart hammers against my chest. I don't know if I can continue to move slowly. God how I want you. God, how I always want you."

"Go on."

"'No bruises in sight,' I say, and with my thumbs

I brush the nipples trapped inside the lace."

Sadie moaned.

"They harden like nuggets of gold beneath my touch and I rub them back and forth. . ." Sebastian stops for a minute. Imagining Sadie rubbing herself for him was too much. His cock pushed against his jeans and he swallowed. Control. He needed to keep control. He wanted to do this for her.

"And I have to lie still?"

"Very still." His voice sounded ragged with desire. She would know how turned on he was and that turned him on more. "Sadie…"

"Keep going Doctor. Your touch is so healing."

"My hands slide down to your waist. They tremble as I undo the button and zipper of your pants. I slide them down your unbelievably long legs. Sculpted, I swear, in heaven. Your body is sending me beyond…" He took a breath. "I throw your pants to the floor."

"And what about my thong?"

Oh shit. Her thong. Her white, lace thong. The one he bought her in a boutique in Florence. The one she wore for their special nights. "Sadie," he whispered.

"You're undoing me."

"Your touch is gentle, but firm, sensitive, yet demanding. I don't know you, but that no longer matters. I want you," she said.

"My hand slides to your sex and finds you moist. But I want you wetter, much, much wetter."

Sadie groaned. "Can I do anything yet?"

"No."

"Nothing."

"Hey, I started this fantasy. I get to call the shots. I'm touching your mouth with my hand now, to still you from talking."

She giggled.

"Now my left hand is trailing down from your face to your nipple as my right slides under your thong and explores your soft, wet folds." The memory of how they felt gave him a sharp rush. "You feel so warm and inviting, so feminine and alluring, so ready. I increase the pressure of my fingers and run them along you, slowly at first and then as your clit rises I stroke it."

"I move my lower body upwards to meet your hand. It feels so good. I want more."

Sadie's breathing stepped up and she made a mewing sound. "My other hand teases you rock-hard nipple and your back arches."

Sadie moaned.

"You're ready for me now, but I want to torment you. I want to torture you with desire."

"Sebastian." She sounded more than ready.

"I want you, all of you. I want to push into your heat until we both explode. I can't wait any longer."

"I want you now," she said.

"I climb onto the table and hover over you. I pull your legs apart and lower my mouth on top of you, tasting your heat, your sweet, sweet heat. You call out."

"Sebastian." The need for him in her voice— almost too much.

"My tongue. . ."

"Shit." She interrupted him. " I can't."

"What?"

"It's Cole... On my phone... I can't ignore this call. Not after what happened this morning." Panting. "I'm so sorry. We were so close."

Her words hit him like a fucking glacier. "Damn, I

hate doing it on the phone. We keep getting interrupted."

"We'll make up for it, in person," she said. "I promise." She used a sultry voice she knew he liked.

He exhaled noisily. "Soon, baby, soon."

Silence.

"Gotta go…" She clicked off.

CHAPTER FOUR

"What the hell, Sadie." Cole sounded angry.

When Sadie picked up the call, she expected to hear Cole's usual salutation, "How are you doing sugar," spoken with a distinct southern drawl, but not today.

"Don't blame me." She had heard her handler angry before, but never quite this angry. She smiled. It was kind of fun to rankle the savvy master spy's cool. It made him seem almost human. Almost. She tried to slow her breathing. Sebastian had set her on fire and now she had to talk to her boss.

"You shot a drone in a public park in New York and you didn't call me."

"I was going to. . ." But given the choice of hot sex

or a reprimand from her boss, she had chosen sex. Her cheeks still burned with pleasure. "I had to get Beatrice and the dog back to safety. Then I called and you were in a meeting with the big-wigs, so I sent you a text. I was just about to phone you again."

Cole went quiet. Not a good thing. She imagined him at the headquarters of the CIA in Langley, dressed in a Wall Street suit with a well-pressed white shirt open at the color, sitting in his well-worn office chair. Every strand of his salt-and-pepper hair would be in place. His steely gray eyes would be scanning the monitors on the wall as he spoke, not losing a detail of the global information passing before him. His desk would be well-organized: a laptop, a cup of Earl Grey tea and a small chessboard with a game in play. No paper. Cole was an enigma of a man and liked it that way. Scary at close range and scarier now he was mad.

"Cole?"

He grunted. "Sadie, you were on a call to Sebastian. Do you think I wouldn't know that?"

Fudge. Double Fudge. Double fudge sundae with a cherry on top. He knows who I'm talking to?

Did he know what they were doing?

A rush of anger rose within her constricting her throat and her thoughts, but she beat it down, reminding herself that while the intrusiveness of the CIA could be annoying at times, it had also saved her life. She swallowed. "I needed to talk to him."

"I told you to break it off."

"I tried."

"How's that going?"

"Not so well, Jeremiah." She used his first name on purpose, hoping to break through the hard crust of the weathered spy-master and reach the heart of a real man. "I love him."

"It doesn't matter. You have to end it." He grumbled. "But now is not the time to be talking about your love life. Who targeted you?"

"No idea." She told him the details of the event, clearly, succinctly and without emotion, the way he had trained her to report.

Silence resumed. Fucking silence. He knew too much about her life. Way too much. Probably knew how many thongs she owned. She bit her lip. "It's *them*, again?"

"Most likely." Cole never guessed. He took in information like a computer, analyzed it and came to a hypothesis. He was rarely wrong. In the business he was known for having good hunches, but she knew they were never really hunches; they were well-processed concepts.

"What do the police know?" She knew he would have already talked to them.

"Not much. They've collected a few cell-phone pictures and videos from people who were there. So far they have only found one that has an identifiable image of you on it, and it has been taken care of."

"Thank you. I've told Beatrice to keep quiet about it."

She swore she could hear him nod.

"There's no new intel on the KOTL, but I have an operative working on developing a relationship with an inside man"

Sadie pulled a hand through her hair. "Someone has to know something."

Cole probably winced at the overused line, right

out of a cheesy B movie with a mystery theme. She had thought last Christmas of giving him a plaque with the saying on it, for his office, just to bug him.

After a moment, he said, "I need you in one piece."

"My, my. Is that affection in your voice or do you need another cup of tea?"

He grunted. "Take all precautions, sugar." He clicked off.

Sadie hit the shower. All precautions? Of course she would. Who wouldn't after someone tried to kill them? And it wasn't the first time. And she was a trained operative. What's with Cole? The hot water on her aching muscles felt so good it slowed her rant and for a few minutes of bliss she let the crazy world spin on its own.

When she slipped on her robe, reality slipped back into her brain. She tried to count the number of times Cole had used the take-precaution line on her. It was a common term in the business and she knew what he meant by it, but it bothered her. She wrapped towel around her hair and put it on top of her head, like a turban. Shit. He'd never used that line on her before. Coffee. She needed caffeine.

Her company phone rang. Jeremiah wasn't the chatty type. What could he want now?

After she clicked her phone on, she said, "I'm still wet from my shower."

"So?"

"What is it, Cole?"

"I've been reading through the KOTL file, wondering how you could possibly be linked to them."

"And..."

"Did your mother leave you any stuff?"

Sadie swallowed. Her mother had died ten years ago, on a wet Seattle night, when a drunk driver in a big SUV skipped the center line on the I-5 and plowed straight into her. A head-on. She didn't have a chance. She winced at the memory of that night. Damn, she hated talking about her mother. An alcoholic with many a sad tale to tell, she had not had much of a life. Death had been the last lousy-break in a life of lousy breaks for her. She gathered them like a magnet, but Sadie knew better than anyone that her mother was a good woman at heart. Just fragile and worn from her journey. Sadie loved her then and now. She just preferred to not talk about her. "Stuff?"

"You know, family mementos."

"My mother didn't collect anything that required dusting. She threw out every picture I drew for her. And there sure as hell were no family jewels. If there had been she would have sold them for booze." She hesitated, "But. . ." The image came to her mind.

"What?"

"She did keep an old chest in her closet. A big, blue metal one with a lock on it. I used to imagine it held secrets."

"Did it?"

"I took a brief look into it before I put it into storage ten years ago. It has photograph books and some old papers. Nothing important." As she spoke an eerie sense of knowing trickled through her mind and down her spine. She shivered.

"Where is the chest now?"

"In a storage unit in Seattle."

"Give me the details. I'll send someone to open it

up and take a look."

"No." She didn't mean to say it so loudly. It wasn't her place to command. "I. . . I don't want anyone in her things. Have them send it to me." She gave him the address of the storage company. Would he respect her privacy? Mmm, maybe.

"It will be sent today."

"Thanks Jeremiah."

"Sugar," he said in his honey dipped southern drawl, "be careful."

CHAPTER FIVE

April 2

The next morning at ten, a man wearing jeans low enough on his hips to make her eyes linger down *there,* where no woman likes to be caught looking in public, delivered her mother's chest. Pulling her eyes up his body, she tried hard not to stall on his killer smile. *It should be banned by the Global Warming initiative.* She could fault herself at noticing his good looks, but as her best friend Mitch liked to say, "No harm in window shopping." The man was a gorgeous hunk of humanity.

Looking at him, perhaps too closely, Sadie stood in her doorway, with her right hand on her gun in the pocket of her robe. No makeup, no shoes—a bit of a disaster. She felt drabber than drab. Why did Cole send this Greek God guy?

The answer clicked into her mind: because he wanted to distract her. Get her away from Sebastian. Her mouth broke into a big smile. *Nice try Jeremiah.*

The man's green eyes looked her over without apology. Undoubtedly, he knew her code name was Mata Hari, and had heard stories, possibly many stories about her escapades. The unmistakable, carnal heat in his gaze put the question in the air.

Was she interested in a morning romp with a handsome stranger?

Running a hand through her mane of hair, she gave him a pleasant smile, the kind you give your kid brother when he's washed your car for you. "Let's get on with it," she said.

He nodded. "Have the cherry blossoms bloomed?"

Which moron came up with these lines? "On the streets of Seattle," she replied.

"Never had a flower line before." His voice low and all too inviting made her feel like a woman wanted by a man, but there was only one man for her.

Sadie opened the door wider and he brought the chest into her apartment. "You can put it there for me," she said pointing to the spot right in front of her sofa. "Thank you."

The smell of his leather jacket lingered after he left, as did the image in her head of what she had turned down.

But what secrets hid in her mother's treasure chest? An old piece of luggage, it looked weathered and beaten as she expected, but smaller than she remembered. In her imagination it had been large enough to contain all the family secrets, all their pasts. In reality it was about two by three feet, made of battered, cheap metal and felt cold to the touch.

She'd seen it before, many times, but the palms of her hands sweated. *Get a grip, Sadie. You've handled killers and arms-dealers and... you can handle a box.* But family secrets can hit harder than anything else in the world. Secrets remain hidden for a reason. Did she want to know all of them?

The old-fashioned, high-school combination lock

was still in place. That made her smile. If the CIA had tampered with it, they had done a fine job of putting it back in place. Maybe Cole had respected her on this.

With trembling fingers she worked the lock using the combination she remembered: the year of her mother's birth, the year of her own birth and the year the Seattle Seahawks joined the NFL. She pulled down and the lock opened. Sadie swallowed.

The lid lifted easily and she peered inside for the first time in ten years. After her mother's death, she had been too paralyzed by grief to delve into it. After she packed all her mother's things and donated them to the Salvation Army, she had intended to go through this box. But she put it off, figuring she could do it later. Then later grew and it ended up in storage. Someday, she told herself, she would go through it and save the old pictures of her mother.

With the chest open, the faint smell of Lily of the Valley, her mother's favorite perfume, rose into the air. A tsunami of memories flooded Sadie's mind. Sweet Jesus, it would be easier to face a firing squad than this box. She bit her lip. What had her mother kept hidden all those years? She knelt on the floor in front of the chest gathering her determination which threatened to seep away from her.

Her chest tightened. It was as if she was a little girl again and her mother was in the next room. Only she wasn't little anymore, and her mother wasn't, and never would be, in the next room.

Shit. She needed to be focused and calm. She would think of it as an assignment. Her life might rely on it. Gritting her teeth, she pulled out an old, blue, silk scarf her mother used to wear on special occasions, a treasured present from her father. Soft and elegant, just like her mother. Tears trickled down her face. Sadie tried to rub them away with the back of her hand, but they kept coming. *Why did my mother have to die so young? It wasn't fair.*

Life isn't fair, Sadie. Get on with it. Beneath the scarf sat an odd collection of things, layered in a haphazard pattern. Sadie decided to pull them out one by one. On the right side three photo albums had been stacked on top of one another. She pulled them out and set them on the coffee table to look through later. A life could not be summed up in three albums, but they were all that was left. Her breathing caught. Later, she would look later.

On the left side of the trunk, sat a pink, velvet, jewelry box, which once belonged to her grandmother. Opening it, she found her mother's wedding rings and an assortment of favorite necklaces and a set of origami, swan earrings. Sadie remembered those earrings well. She had made them for her mother when she was twelve. She held them up to the light. She had no idea her mother treasured them so much.

Underneath the jewelry box lay her grandfather's, fisherman-knit sweater. She pulled it to her nose to breathe in his familiar scent: wood smoke, salt and a touch of after-shave. As she pulled the wool garment close to her, a brown, leather-bound book tumbled to the ground.

She had never seen this book before and when she touched it, she knew it was what she was looking for. That made no sense, but she knew. She just knew.

Written on the first page: "Emma-Mae's journal 1913-1915." That would be right around the time of the

First World War.

Emma-Mae? That would have been her great-aunt on her mother's side, her grandmother's spinster sister. Hmm. Her mother rarely spoke of her family, but she did know this aunt was considered a bit strange. Never married, never "conformed" as her mother said. The woman lived a wild life as a flapper and travelled around the world with men. Her independence hadn't sat well with the family, which had been as old-fashioned, waspy as they come. Fun of any kind was kept strictly at arm's length, because it might let the devil in, and all that crap. But Emma-Mae's life had intrigued Sadie.

Turning randomly to a page, she noted the woman had beautiful handwriting, a lost art. Dated Sept. 4, 1915, the entry said:

"I've been sent to Egypt to pick up a parcel, but as usual they aren't telling me what's in the parcel."

An awareness hit Sadie like a hammer between the eyes.

CHAPTER SIX

Leon examined his technical drawings for Avenger. Through years of study at MIT and work in his own lab, he had mastered more than the basics of robotics. His killing machine should have worked and yet a single, well aimed shot exploded it into a million pieces. But then how could he have predicted she would have a gun? Perhaps if he had increased its speed once it recognized her.

Perhaps. What did it matter? He failed. Again. He was a failure. A useless, over-educated idiot. Those were just some of the names his father had used over the phone. Leon put his glass of cognac down on the table. How could he fix things?

He wanted to strangle Sadie Stewart with his

bare hands, but knew he didn't have the stomach for violence. He had trouble killing flies. Sending out Avenger had been more difficult than anything he had ever done. It had required a lot of cognac and endless rationalization.

Leon didn't want to kill her, or anyone else for that matter. Murder wasn't in his blood. He picked up his cell phone and punched in his father's private cell number.

"Have you killed her yet?"

"About that."

"God damn it. Don't think. Do it."

"I'm not good at killing people. We should hire someone who is good at it."

"Let me remind you. If you don't kill her, I'm cutting you off."

The silence lasted longer than he wanted it to. "Father?"

"Son, you have more at stake than you know."

"What do you mean? You've already threatened my income and my inheritance. What else is there?"

"You must understand. You have to kill her."

"I don't have to do anything."

"The KOTL take care of loose ends. If you don't succeed, you will become a loose end. If you want to live, you must kill the woman. If you fail, you will be killed."

"A loose end?"

"I will not be able to protect you. You must kill the woman."

"What if I found another way?"

"There is no other way, son. You must kill her and there must be proof that she is dead."

CHAPTER SEVEN

Once Sadie opened Emma-Mae's journal

she couldn't stop reading. She started at the beginning:

∞

February – 1913

Dearest Diary,

God that sounds awful. Sappy and overly sentimental as if I were the type of person who would keep a journal about their life! Diaries are for mothers who want to relish in the memories of childrearing, or retired Generals who want to relive their victories. I am not a mother or a general.

They write with the belief that someday their descendants will want to read about their lives. Rather narcissistic, but there you have it. I imagine their writing makes them feel more important, more whole, more engaged with the universe and the meaning of life.

I have no stories about my baby's first steps, or how to

make my husband's favorite meal. Nor do I have stories about arranging an army for battle.

No this will not be a normal diary.

Let me introduce myself. I am Emma-Mae Jones, daughter of Edgar Jones, a clerk in a barrister's office in London who died too young to achieve his main ambition of becoming a lawyer himself. My mother, Elouisa Mae Jones, is a bit of a puzzle to me. She refuses to talk about her past and now survives in a small flat in London. I send her money regularly. I have one sister, Elizabeth, who is much more normal than me and determined to be married soon.

I'm thirty years old, an old maid. I spend my days doing many different things. How can I say this? Some days I am courtesan. I'm told, I'm good at that. Other days I am an executive secretary. I stink at that. My number sense isn't the best and I make weak tea. Some days I am an old woman's companion. I'm a chameleon by nature and trade. I do not wish to incriminate myself, but nor do I wish to fall into the trap of believing in any of the masks I wear.

I am a spy.

∞

Sadie put her finger in the book, leaned back and laughed. *Unbelievable.* Her great-aunt Emma-Mae had been a spy. How could Sadie not have known the truth about her?

Clearly, the profession of espionage ran deep in her blood. A tingling sensation ran up her spine. Sadie put down the book, grabbed a pen and a piece of paper and started drawing a genealogical map. Edgar and Elouisa-Mae Jones of London had two daughters, Emma-Mae and Elizabeth. Elizabeth Jones married Winston Parker and emigrated to the States where they had five children. One of those children was Sadie's mother, Pearl. Yes, that made Emma-Mae her great-aunt. Her mother had only mentioned the woman once or twice and the comments had been in hushed tone. Sadie tried to recall what exactly her mother had said.

Her last memory came to mind. It was a cold November night and Sadie was twelve. Her mother lay semi-conscious on the sofa, having drunk too much whiskey. Worried she might catch cold, Sadie placed a blanket on top of her. As she did so, her mother said, "Just like my Aunty Emma-Mae."

Sadie tucked the blanket in around her mother's body to keep her warm. "My aunty used to tuck me in like this when she came to visit." Sadie had asked her to tell her more. "Oh she was a wild woman and she had many adventures. But I wasn't allowed to listen to her stories. My mother said she lacked morals." Sadie grinned at the memory. *Gotta read more.* She opened the journal again.

Emma-Mae wrote:

∞

War is imminent. I feel angry and frustrated not being able to do anything about it. As I complained to my friend Annie, she simply said, "I have the perfect job for you." I remember feeling my eyes pop open. I had never had a perfect job, or for that matter any that I liked at all. Then she added, "But it would be dangerous."

∞

Emma-Mae had her hooked.

∞

"They,"—and I won't give you details as to who "they" are— started me slowly. I would be sent places to pick up packages and bring them back. It was easy. Then they sent me to find out things from this person or that. Again, easy. I have a natural talent for listening and people like to tell me things. I noticed they were sending me to talk to men more than women.

∞

Sadie's company phone buzzed. She put the book down and picked it up. Cole's familiar numeric code ran across the top. She clicked it on.

"Morning, sugar," he said with his southern drawl warm enough to soften butter.

She waited. Damn him for calling. She wanted to read the diary.

"Got your text," he prompted.

Oh yeah. She squeezed her shoulders up and down and stretched her back. Being so involved in Emma-Mae's story, she had forgotten that she sent him a text to tell him that she had received the chest. "I was just reading it," she said.

"Reading what?"

"Oh, that's right. I haven't told you what I found." She proceeded to tell him the details.

He snickered. Sadie had only heard him laugh about three times since she met him. "I know, I know— a spy in the family. Who would have guessed," she said.

"I'll do some research." Something in the tone of his voice bothered her.

Sadie listened closely to intonations in voices, a skill that had saved her life many times. It wasn't in the cadence of Cole's speech, or in the words he chose. It was the tone—silent but deadly cold.

What did Cole know? Damn him. She'd bet her Mother's, silk scarf he knew more than he was saying. She took a deep breath as her body kicked into a sudden state of alertness. Damn the "need-to-know" world of spies. He knew something.

"Why wouldn't my great-aunt show up when they did a background check on me?" she asked.

"The lady could have been a master spy, sugar. They rarely hit the radar. And if they do, their tales are not recorded on paper."

With that he clicked off. Was that the answer? Her great-aunt had been so adept at spy craft she left no traces. Or had she been so complicit in international affairs that any trace of her had been extinguished long ago? Or? She looked at the cell phone, then her great-aunt's book. A chill ran through her to the marrow of her bones. Maybe Cole did know. Maybe the whole company knew. Had she been played from the moment she signed up? For that matter, had they sought her out?

She ran a hand through her hair. *Living in a world of suspicion sucks.*

CHAPTER EIGHT

Sadie looked at her cell phone for a minute

as if it held the answers and then she laughed at herself.

No technology was that good. She thought back to the

assassination attempt the day before. When did she

first see the drone? What faces were in the crowd?

What could she have done differently? She groaned.

The last thing she needed was the New York City Police

knocking on her door

As if on cue, someone knocked on the door. She

opened the door for Beatrice. Casanova jumped up on

her and she stumbled back for a second. They had

worked hard to train him, but while he would indulge

them by sitting, staying and lying down on command,

he couldn't seem to master the art of saying polite

hellos. "They" included four of them: Beatrice, Sadie's best friend Mitch, Sebastian and herself. When Casanova spied one of his pack he hadn't seen for awhile, he would run full speed as if his life depended on it, jump up on them, place his large paws on their shoulders and thoroughly lick their face. It could be most inconvenient at times, but today it felt just right. She laughed. "Down Cassy. Down."

He complied, but with his tail waving frantically he looked like a squirmy ragdoll. Sadie scratched the top of his head and gave him a dog bone. Devouring it in one easy gulp, he looked up at her for more, as if she never fed him. Why did she worry about what flavor to buy him when he never took the time to taste them? She shook her head.

"How you doing?" asked Beatrice. Her cheeks were a little pinker than usual, but not one hair on her head had fallen out of place. She smelled, as usual, of peppermints.

Sadie waggled her head from side to side. "I don't like being chased by robotic monsters."

"I thought you might like Cassy for company."

Sadie laughed. "He could lick an attacker to death." It had become their tag line for Cassy, whose friendly demeanor made him a lousy, guard dog, but a wonderful buddy.

"You never know. If someone tried to hurt you, he might find a growl in him."

"Growls don't stop drones." But Sadie felt the tug of a smile on her lips. Her neighbor and her dog. She couldn't find better companions.

"You want company, or you got stuff to do?" Beatrice's blue-gray eyes, the color of a stormy-night sky, peered over her spectacles.

"Look, Beatrice, you won't tell anyone?"

"Not a chance, honey. Your secret is safe with me."

Sadie touched the woman's hand. "You know you're a stubborn old bat. You should have left the park when I told you to."

"Right," Bee said. A smile lit up her wrinkled face. "So you said."

Sadie hugged her. There didn't seem to be enough words to express how grateful she felt to have

Beatrice in her life. "I'll take Cassy for a walk. That should calm me down."

"Bullshit. You're as calm, cool and collected as they come. You can't fool me, Cheekbones. So stop trying. You're going back to see what you can find out. Be careful."

Sadie winked at her. "Cassy, come," she said.

The dog looked up from the piece of rawhide he'd found under the kitchen table. He picked his treat up in his mouth and stood, upsetting the table and knocking everything on it over. The salt shaker rolled right off onto the floor. The china, tea pot fell on its side and tea poured out, all over her new table cloth.

Sadie winced. Why did she decide she needed a dog? But when he nudged her side and looked at her with those molten brown eyes, she remembered.

***

A couple hours later Sadie and Casanova returned to the apartment. Sadie had run out of dog cookies, and without them walking with Cassy became a tug-of-war.

The area where the drone exploded remained cordoned off, so she hadn't learned much, but they had enjoyed the spring day. Cassy had smelled at least one hundred construction posts and for the most part had stayed at heel.

After putting on her espresso machine, she checked in with Cole. The conversation was brief. No news there.

It took time to gather facts. Waiting for them could be hell. She ran her hand through her hair. Tomorrow, she had a photo shoot. She needed to rest to look fresh. Her phone rang. Sebastian's name scrolled across the display. Good timing. But then, Sebastian always had good timing.

***

Sadie dropped Cassy off with Beatrice at six the next morning and grabbed a taxi to her shoot. An inch of makeup and hair spray transformed her into the image Le Mouton Noir wanted to sell their new line of cashmere: sophisticated, sultry and sexy. As the cameras flashed, she worked her magic, pouting into the camera with her lips as she kept her eyes still and remote, as if to say, you can look at me, but you can't touch me. That look made sold her as a model and provided a nice cover for her spy-life.

Despite everyone's hard work, the shoot went on, and on, and on into the evening. Sadie got back to her apartment at eight. Her plan was to shower, pick up Cassy and spend a quiet evening resting her feet. Maybe she'd have time to finish reading the Toni Anderson book she had started. Once inside, she found an envelope on the floor. Someone must have slid it beneath the door. A note was tucked inside. Who used paper these days? As she kicked the door closed, she slipped open the sheet of paper. The note read:

Sadie,

I've taken Cassy to the vet emergency. I'll call you when I know something.

Beatrice that's who uses paper. She remembered now. The woman refused to use smart phones. or stupid phones for that matter, claiming they let Big Brother follow her every move; a paranoia probably not far from the truth considering her long run with a Vegas mob. Cassy. Poor Cassy.

Below the message Bee had scribbled the address of a familiar emergency clinic. Sadie had taken Cassy there a couple of months ago when he had stepped on a piece of glass and his paw wouldn't stop bleeding. He probably did that again, or maybe he gobbled up some garbage that didn't agree with him. Sebastian called him a Dogerator, as in a dog-garberator, because of his love for eating any garbage left around, including her favorite thong, Sebastian's sock and the skeleton of a twenty pound Chinook salmon. And that was only the stuff she knew about.

No matter how tightly they supervised him, his nose got him into trouble. At least she liked the clinic Bee had chosen. Clean and efficient. Everything would be okay, or so she told herself   as her heart beat rose loud enough to pulse in her throat. Her baby was sick, or wounded.

On her personal cell, Sadie checked her contacts, found the number for the clinic and clicked it. A call came in and Beatrice's name scrolled across the top. She stopped her outgoing call and picked up the incoming one from Beatrice.

"I have bad news." Beatrice's tobacco-worn voice had an extra edge to it.

"What happened?"

"They don't know. I don't know. Cassy started vomiting and wouldn't stop. I brought him in and they're running tests on him."

"Did you go out today?"

"Just for our usual morning stroll. Maybe twenty minutes."

"Was he ever out of your sight?"

The line went quiet for a couple of seconds. "No, but when I came home I had a feeling."

Sadie waited, and a second later when she couldn't wait any longer she asked, "Had someone been in your apartment?"

"I think so. It wasn't that anything was messed up. But it was just a feeling I had, that my space had been invaded and there was a faint smell of cinnamon. You know I don't cook."

"Any of your fellas?" Beatrice had a number of guy friends.

"No. This wasn't a pleasant smell."

"Did Cassy eat after he came home?"

"No he had already eaten, so I didn't give him more. He lay down on his mat and chewed a rawhide."

"New rawhide?"

"Yeah."

"Do you have it with you?"

"No. It's in my apartment. You don't think. . ."

"I haven't given him a new rawhide for a week. Have you?"

"No."

***

Breathing deeply to the count of five, Sadie dashed off messages to Cole and Sebastian. "Cassy poisoned. Going to vets office." And she gave the address. Sadie wanted more than her next breath to run directly to Casanova's side, but she had to proceed with care. Someone could be using him to get to her. She fought back tears. Poor Cassy. He didn't deserve this.

As she entered the elevator, her phone rang. "Caller unknown" ran across the top of the screen of her personal mobile. She clicked it open:

"If you want the antidote to the poison your dog

ingested, you need to meet me."

"What will the poison do to him?"

"Slowly," and he said the word slowly, "and painfully, it will shut down his vital organs, one by one, until he dies."

"How long?"

"Ten hours."

"Ten?" A cold trickle of sweat slid down her spine.

"The experts could be wrong. He could have less." He paused for a second and then continued, "I want to meet you. We have important matters to discuss."

Like my death? "When and where?" she replied.

"Now, at the park. Don't be stupid. Don't tell anyone. I want you alone. If you take more than twenty minutes to arrive, I will know you have alerted the police or someone else."

She would have to jog to get there in twenty. The creep was right. There was no time to send a written message or phone anyone. But what the asshole didn't know was that there was enough time for her to hit the distress button on her company phone. Cole would track her and send reinforcements. Turning her back to the camera in the top corner of the elevator car, she retrieved the black cell from her purse and hit the button. The doors opened and she started running.

The only advantage she had, or might have, was that her hunter didn't know who he was dealing with. At least she could hope he would underestimate her.

CHAPTER NINE

Sadie ran five blocks through crowded

sidewalks to Bryant Park. Sweat streamed down her
face. Her heart banged against her chest, but not from
the aerobic activity. Good Lord she loved that dog. The
thought of losing him, of him not being at home to meet
her when she came to New York, shattered her; made
her feel small, weak and victimized. Shit, some tough
spy she turned out to be.

Sadie had never had a pet before. The bond that
formed between her and Cassy was stronger than she
thought possible, even though she shared him with
others. She snickered. Cole worried she cared too much
for Sebastian. Here she was running into the muzzle of
an assassin's gun to save a mutt with raw meat from the

garbage breath.

A lovable mutt, mind you. A wet nosed, fluffy haired, tail wagging mutt who adored his masters.

Sadie arrived and scanned the area. The park looked much as it had the day she and Beatrice had come to play bridge. People wandered about doing their thing on the warm evening.

One man stood out. He wore a trench coat worthy of a cold war movie!

Really? Would her assailant be that obvious? No one else in the park looked odd, or at least no more odd than normal.

No one appeared to be looking towards him. But good back-up would be hard to see at first glance.

Slowing her pace, she checked her watch. She'd made it with thirty seconds to spare. How could she stall the meet?

That's when she saw Mabel, Beatrice's friend, the one with the pinched face, who had come to play bridge on Wednesday. Sadie jogged over to her.

"Hi, Mabel."

The woman had thin, white hair pulled back into a low pony tail and wore a no-nonsense pant suit. Sadie remembered Bee telling her once that this woman wrote technical manuals. She looked it. When the woman recognized her, she said, "You."

"Look, I need a favor."

"I know. I know, already. Beatrice told us not to tell the cops about you. I won't, sweetie. I know what it's like to hide from an asshole husband."

Sadie's brows shot up.

"Don't you worry. Beatrice told us all about how your ex-husband kidnapped you in Amsterdam."

Sadie smiled. Bee knew how to get her friends to cooperate. And the story was true; but Jonathon, her asshole-ex, hadn't bothered her since that day. His mother and Sebastian had seen to that. He wouldn't dare interfere with her life again. But Mabel didn't need to know that. " Yes, well, see that guy over there in the beige trench coat?" Sadie tilted her head towards the man.

Mabel turned and looked in the direction Sadie indicated. "The one who looks like Columbo?"

"Yeah."

"I think he's following me."

The woman looked back at Sadie with narrow eyes. "What can I do?"

"I'd like you to go up and talk to him, distract him,so that I can get closer and get a better look."

"What will I talk to him about?"

"Tell him you lost your cat and start describing him."

Mabel firmed her jaw and nodded. "I can do that."

"And ramble. That will give me more time."

She nodded.

"And if you run out of things to say, pretend to faint."

A mischievous smile crossed Mabel's face, lightening her features by a century. "This could be fun."

As Mabel headed off on her mission, Trench-Coat-Guy turned and looked in Sadie's direction. Nowhere to hide.

She wanted to take his picture, but couldn't risk

it. *Memorize his ugly face, Sadie. Memorize his face.* Five-ten, medium build, no hair visible beneath the brown fedora, white skin, Coke bottle glasses with tortoise-shell frames, dark eyes. Tilted mustache.

The steady groan of a helicopter's engine caught her attention. *Yay, the cavalry's coming.* She looked up. Maybe not. She recognized the logo of a local TV news station on its side. Cole had friends everywhere and many of them owed him favors, but he hated the media more than he hated losing his queen on the chessboard. She decided to hang on to the possibility the copter was coming to help her.

Trench-coat-guy looked toward the sky for a second. Then Mabel poked his arm and he jumped. Squaring her shoulders in front of him, she started talking and waving her arms in the air like a manic humming bird. Bless her heart. The woman was more effective than a machine gun. The man's mouth dropped open and he took a step back.

Sadie scanned the area one more time. Seeing nothing out of the ordinary, she moved closer to them.

"Look lady I haven't seen your calico cat and I

don't wanna see him. Shove off."

"If I've lost Dausy, I don't know what I'd do."
Mabel's voice had a tightly wound, fragility to it, that
made her sound as if she herself might break at any
moment.

The man put his hands on his hips. No visible
weapons. Sadie walked around him and approached
from behind. She grabbed one of his arms and twisted it
up.

"Ow. Shit. What the hell?"

Sadie pulled harder on his arm, making his body
lurch an inch forward.

Mabel stopped talking. So did the man.

Out of nowhere a policeman appeared at her
side. "Black bishop takes pond."

"J'adoube," she replied, using the chess term for
adjustment. Only Cole would send in a man with a chess
password. Her shoulders relaxed.

"What would you like me to do with him?" he
asked as he pulled cuffs from his belt.

The helicopter hovered above them now. The
side door opened and a man leaned out with binoculars.

He looked military, dressed in army fatigues. Definitely not the evening news camera man. She gave him a thumbs-up and as he retreated back inside, the helicopter moved away.

The cavalry had come, but the damn, prickly sensation at the nape of her neck held on. She looked around. Three men dressed in black suits came forward. She recognized them as company men and they looked it, hiding behind tinted glasses.

Trench-coat-guy started squirming. "Hey, lady, I don't know what this is about. I didn't take this woman's cat. I swear. I'm innocent."

As the men moved in, Sadie released his arm.

Rubbing his shoulder, he turned around to face her. Sweat beaded on his brow. It smelled rancid with a tinge of fried, greasy onions and a whole lot of fear.

"What do you want?" he said, looking at her with eyes so jumpy they could hardly hold her gaze. "Listen, I don't know what you're all so upset about. A guy paid me to put on a trench coat and a mustache and stand in the park. He gave me a hundred bucks, said it was a joke. No crime in that."

"Just to stand here?"

He reached for his pocket and all of them reached for their guns. "No, no! I just want to get a note for you. He said to give it to the pretty red-head."

Sadie winced. Could he have an arsenic capsule like the guy in Venice? He didn't have cold vibe of an assassin or the confidence, but she wouldn't take the chance. "Put both your hands in the air and hold still," she said. Sliding her hand into his pocket, she found an envelope, about the size of a small greeting card and pulled it out. Sealed.

Taking a step back, she wondered if it could be poisoned. But hell Cassy's life was at stake. Without another thought she opened it:

Dear Ms. Stewart,

I see you have met my messenger. I am watching. I know how many friends you brought. Tsk tsk. So unladylike to lie, my dear.

I was sent to kill you, and I understand I'm not your first. I think it would be mutually beneficial for us to meet.

Perhaps we could come up with a plan to satisfy

the people who sent me and keep you alive.

I suspect you would prefer to live. There must be some way to settle this score.

Please join me for a late dinner at Jimmy's Steak House on the west side. No goons.

If you arrive by ten, the antidote to the poison I used on your dog will be sent to the vet clinic. All you have to do is turn up—alone.

Looking up at the men, she said, "Let him go. I've got what I want and he's harmless." She turned, waved good-bye to Mabel who she would talk to later and started running home.

Sadie had two hours to figure things out. Her company phone buzzed, but she ignored it. Saving Cassy was her goal.

CHAPTER TEN

Sadie kicked the door closed behind her.

Ninety minutes until her meet. What could she find out in that short a time?

"*Mijn liefje.*" The voice as smooth, sexy and potent as a shot of whisky at midnight came from Sebastian whose long, lean and perfect body lay stretched out on the sofa.

She sighed. "Sebastian?"

"Come here." He opened her arms.

Damn, she didn't have time for this. But double damn, she sure wanted time for this. She walked over and stood above him. "What are you doing here?"

As his blue eyes softened, her mouth went dry.

Shouldn't she be able to control her desire for him by now? The twinge in her lower belly answered that thought. *Obviously not.*

"I told you, I'm alright," she said, leaving some distance between them. "And I'm sweaty."

He shrugged. "I like hot women. And, I get you. An assassin is stalking you and you're feeling. . . What is the English term for it— Dandy?"

"Yup, just dandy. That's me." They both as Seb stood up. He looked even better standing. Like a Norse God, a giant of a man made of lean, hard muscle. As he closed the distance between them, her heart beat loud enough for the UN to hear it. *Control Sadie. You need control.*

"Any contact with the asshole?" he asked.

Sweat trickled down her neck. Her breathing sped. *Oh hell. Why waste time on words.* "Is that what's on your mind?" She stepped closer to him.

He gave her a wicked grin and pulled her into his strong arms. His rugged, manly smell mixed with the scent of spicy after-shave melted the last of her resolve. His mouth took hers and her whole world tilted. Dear

God, no man should be able to kiss like that. Tender, loving, passionate... She pushed him away. "Sebastian, I can't"

He kissed her neck. "Stop thinking. You need this. You need us."

Desire coiled within her body. "I have things to do..." He kissed her on that sensitive spot in the hollow on her shoulder." "Things to..." Her mind lost its thought. There had been one there a second ago.

"Not now, baby." He picked her up in a swoop, carried her in his arms to the bedroom and placed her gently on the bed.

Sadie liked to have control, but being swept up in his arms never lost its charm. Her body ached for him. Her heart ached for him.

But he didn't jump her, as she expected. Instead, he lay down beside her and propped himself up on one elbow. This was as likely a scenario as being in a lion's den and not getting eaten. She stared at him.

"I have to talk to you," he said.

"Now?" She ran her hand along his arm, tracing his well-developed muscles with her fingertips.

"I've been thinking about how to say it. For days. On the flight over, I decided to just start and the words would find a way."

Is he breaking up with me? Has he had enough of my lifestyle...or? She leaned away from him, as a truly awful thought came to mind. "You have another woman?" They always hit on him.

"Hell no. It's about us—only about us."

He wants to slow things down? Did he feel trapped? He'd never been with one woman for this long. She waited.

"It doesn't matter how long we've known each another."

Sadie opened her mouth to speak, but he put a finger on it to hold it closed.

"It doesn't matter the time of day. It doesn't matter what country each of us is in, I can't get you out of my head." His lips spread into a seductive smile as his fingers slid down her neck to the top button of her blouse.

"That's it?"

"*Godverdomme*, no. But it's a start and the

thought of being inside you. . ." He kissed her lips again—"took over my head. Words can wait."

The gentle touch of his large fingers on her skin made her tremble. As he reached beneath her blouse, her stomach clenched with anticipation. Sebastian had given up on her buttons again. At least he hadn't ripped her blouse this time.

"Let me," she said. In less than a second her blouse flew through the air and fell quietly to the floor like a small, silk parachute. Her pants followed.

The expression of ravenous desire on Sebastian's face lit every cell in her body on fire. He swallowed. The tenderness in his eyes said more than any of his words ever could. He cherished her—beyond words cherished her. She was his woman and his love knew no bounds. All this he communicated in his eyes.

And then there were his fingers... Slowly he traced the lace edge of the top of her bra making a guttural groan that played on her tightly strung libido like a violin bow. Reaching behind her back she unclasped her bra and in a second it catapulted into the air. "We have to be quick. I've got things to do."

"I can do quick." His large hands palmed her breasts, pressing against her hard nipples sending shock waves of pleasure edged with pure lust through her body. No one could turn her on the way he did. No one. He sensed what she wanted and delivered. She moaned as he lowered his mouth to her breasts. She ran her hands through his long, thick hair. Screw Cole. Screw her job. She could never lose Sebastian.

Desire flooded her senses. Her heart beat like a jack-hammer. Two weeks without him had been like an eternity. An eternity without his touch, an eternity without his presence his. . . "Oooooh."

His hand reached beneath her thong and cupped her wet core. She pushed her hips up to meet him. Stroking her with a firmness that drove her wild she rose beyond thought, ready to explode.

But he released his grip and trailed sensuous kisses from her breasts down to her sex. His tongue found her clit and licked it as his finger entered her. Arching her back, she panted, "Now. I want you now."

"Maybe," he said and licked her again stroking her from the inside and out in a rhythm that thrilled her to her core and tightened every fibre of her being. She beat the mattress with her fist.

His touch ...

Moaning, she grabbed his ass. "I want you."

But he didn't stop. "I love you," he said.

Her body and her whole consciousness broke into a million pieces of ecstasy and she screamed his name.

Sebastian crawled up her body and smiled; that killer smile.

Waves of contentment flowed through her, but she still wanted to feel him inside her. Her mind stopped it in a flash. Cassy needed her help.

As if reading her mind, Sebastian said, "It's going to be okay. We'll find an antidote. And when I get my hands on the man who poisoned him. . ." His gentle, lover eyes turned to steel warrior eyes in a flash.

Sadie laughed. "Well look who's becoming a dog person, after all."

"Only for you *mijn liefje*." His mouth took hers and he kissed her deeply.

With the palm of her hand Sadie pushed him off

and rolled on top. "My turn." She loved roving her hands and tongue over his muscled body, but that wasn't quite her plan.

Straddling him, she kissed him hard, determined to show him she had taken control. His large hands grabbed her behind and pressed her to his long, hard erection. She moaned despite her resolve not to enjoy this part.

"I want to try something different," she whispered in his ear.

"Anything you want, baby." His low, gravelly voice sent tingles through her system. *There ought to be a law against this man. Even his voice turns me on.*

"You trust me?" she asked.

"Always."

He's far too good a man for me. She bit her lip as she pulled a pair of handcuffs from the drawer in her bedside table.

Mischief played in Sebastian's eyes. "I didn't think you were into that."

Stroking his length she said, "Why not?"

He sighed, "*Mijn Liefje.*" Again, his sexy voice

threatened to break her resolve, but she clung to the image of Cassy in her mind.

She clicked a cuff to one of his wrists, then lowered the zipper of his jeans freeing his erection. Impressive. She groaned. The thought of having him inside her tormented her senses. *Get a grip Sadie. Get a grip.*

Taking a slow approach would be darn near impossible. He had such a perfect body and she wanted it... Oh how she wanted it. Reaching up to the cuffs, she threaded the middle part behind a post in her headboard. "Give me your other arm," she said.

His brow rose and for a minute she thought he'd make her fight him. "Let me take off my shirt first."

The shirt. Of course. "Good idea. It dropped to the floor and he lay back on the bed. "What next, Sadie?"

Placing his arms above her head, she gave him as wicked a smile as she could muster considering ... Well, considering. With a snap of the lock, his arms were immobilized. Perfect. "All mine to explore. All mine to take. All mine."

Sebastian groaned, which made her swallow her lust. She hadn't expected to get so turned on by making him vulnerable. This had to be one of the most difficult deceptions she had ever tried.

Slowly, she pulled his jeans down his long, toned legs. Every inch of his body excited her. Once the jeans and his shorts were out of the way, she lowered herself to his ankles and licked his skin. Slowly she made her way up to the inside of his loins.

Built like a warrior with a heart of gold, Sebastian aroused feelings in her she didn't think possible. He was her prince, but also her sinful, bad boy. Her man. Her heart thudded in her chest.

How could she keep her mind clear? *Think of the dog, Sadie. Think of the dog.* She looked at her watch. Only ten minutes left to play. She would make the most of them.

Pulling his legs apart she said, "Let's see how still you can lie there." She stroked him as she continued to lick, and taste. Salty, virile man.

He groaned, louder this time, and pulled on the cuffs. They clanked against the metal, but they were standard issue and they would hold.

An unexpected, triumphant feeling of control bubbled inside her. Her nipples hardened. She didn't think having him like this could be so exciting. She stroked him again, and he tilted his head back. "Sadie," he said in a raspy voice.

Her tongue reached the apex of his legs and she explored him thoroughly. His panting increased. Slowly she licked the length of his manhood, and then she took him in her mouth and massaged his other parts. She played with him until he came in one swift, powerful moment.

Shuddering, he sank lower into the bed.

Sadie reached up and kissed him gently on his mouth.

"I want you," he said.

"Later." She pulled away and stood up. "Later, I promise."

"Sadie?"

"I have to go." She jumped off the bed, grabbed her blouse from the floor and threw it on over her head. To hell with the bra. She didn't have time to look for it.

"Sadie?"

"I won't be long." She blew him a kiss.

"*Godverdomme.* At least tell me where are you going?"

"Sebastian, I have to do this on my own."

"I'm here to protect you."

"Sebastian, I don't need your protection." *When would he learn?*

He grunted.

"Lover, you know the saying: 'All is fair in love and… doggy-war.'" He rolled his eyes at her and growled, as she blew him a second kiss. *Time for her date with that scum bag.*

As the bedroom door closed behind her, she heard him mutter, "You'll pay for this."

CHAPTER ELEVEN

Sadie had heard of Jimmy's Steak House

on the west side. It opened a month ago and her friend
Mitch loved it. He said it had great steaks and sexy
waiters, two pluses in his book. The décor, he said, was
so down-home-American he expected to be face-
planted with an apple pie; the kind of place you can eat
comfort food and believe the American dream still
exists, but done so well it met his standard for kitschy.

Tourists come from all over the world to see
New York, all kinds of people, looking for the
quintessential American experience. Who doesn't like a
good steak? Maybe it works. Mitch had tried to get
Sadie to go there, but as part of her new plan to live a

more balanced life she was sticking to a plant- based diet. But tonight she would go there for Cassy.

As Sadie looked at the mock saloon-door entrance, she screwed up her mouth. Maybe Jimmy's was just what it appeared to be, another popular restaurant, not a front for a group of foreign wing-nuts. It didn't look like a trap.

But she was alone.

And he was an assassin.

She could swallow her nervousness, but her mind would not quit. What was she doing confronting the man alone? But the thought of losing Cassy refocused her. She had to meet the drone-master.

Sadie scanned the street one last time. The first thing she learned in the spook business was to expect the unexpected. Did the KOTL have real estate in New York? Possibly. There were so many holes in the information Cole sent her, anything was possible.

Cole. If she were a good girl, she would tell him what she was about to do, but Sadie was not a good girl. Never had been. The image of Sebastian tied to her bed, naked, flickered in her mind's eye. No she wasn't a good girl.

She checked her phone. No calls. 6:55 p.m. Her warning voice screamed at her to stop, but she walked through the door anyway.

Light from the city streamed through the wall of windows in the narrow room. It smelled of beer and people—lots and lots of people—as if it hadn't been aired for months. An old-fashioned, wooden bar looking worn and well-used, framed the back wall. They probably scavenged it from the set of a Western movie. A well-known, country singer Frankie somebody, sang about his unfaithful lover over speakers mounted on the walls.

Sadie took inventory: fifteen small, wooden tables, forty people drinking, mostly beer in large mugs. The patrons came in all colors, textures and styles—a hodgepodge of humanity. It was so all-American-freaking normal and down-home rowdy it prickled her skin.

"Grub upstairs," read the sign hung on the far wall, to the side of the bar. Where was her cowboy hat when needed one? Smiling at her own joke she slipped up the stairs to the second floor with her right hand resting on her gun stashed in her purse.

The second floor smelled of steaks sizzling on the grill. The tables covered in plastic red checkered tablecloths were set off in booths for privacy. Kitchen relics from the last century sat on a high ledge that lined two walls. Below them hung large Norman Rockwell prints of an America everyone wished they lived in, but no one ever had.

In one corner, a young man in denim from head to foot and really cool, cowboy boots, strummed a guitar and sang about making love in his pick-up, his twangy voice barely audible over the chatter of the patrons and the clanging sounds of the kitchen. With the two exits firmly etched in her mind, she tightened her grip on the gun and looked closer at faces.

There were lots of smiling faces and she filed each one into her memory. Then her eyes locked on the man sitting in the corner staring back at her. She nodded at him.

He nodded back.

How do cowboys say, "Bingo?"

Her throat narrowed. But she didn't care. She needed answers.

Cole wouldn't want her meeting an assassin, alone. His sweet, southern drawl would flow over two words: "suicide mission." Well, screw him.

Sebastian definitely wouldn't want her here without him either. He'd be cursing in Dutch right about now. He had to get over it. This meeting was all hers.

Lifting her chin high, she strode across the room.

When she neared his table, he stood and she took a good look at the man who tried to kill her. Mediterranean coloring, a stocky build, dark and murky eyes that showed little emotion. He stood shorter than her, maybe five ten, and wore an expensive, white, dress shirt, perfectly pressed, and black CK slacks. The tilt of his head screamed, "Entitled." He reached his hand out to her. "Leon Krykos the Fourth. Please, sit."

The fourth? Her gut twisted. Over her ten years working as a spy, she had encountered many challenges, played a chameleon a million times over and told hundreds of lies. For that matter, her entire life had become one enormous lie made up of little lies. She had become a living, Russian babushka doll, with layer upon layer of deception. But no deception she had created came near to what she had to do this time. She had to get the better of this man. Cassy's life depended on her manipulation skills. It was no longer a game to beat the bad guy. It was a game to save her dog. She swallowed.

Sadie looked at his outstretched hand. Did she have to shake it? The hand of a man who had tried to kill her? It looked normal enough, but the long fingers, manicured nails, and olive skin covered in curly black hair made her want to retch. She looked askance.

He let his hand fall to his side.

Fixing her eyes on his with a stare meant to be strong enough to bounce off the back of his eyeballs, Sadie sat down opposite him. She fought with the tiny muscles in her face to keep her expression emotionless. "Why do you want to kill me?"

"It's not personal." He shook his head with an arrogant casualness that made her want to pull her gun, shoot and ask his corpse questions. Seriously, nothing is more personal than murder.

"Why then?"

He grimaced, then looked away from her. "I have no choice."

"I see. You have to kill me or..." She let her sentence hang between them while she studied his round brown eyes. They had orange streaks in them, but the lighter color gave them no warmth or depth. They were like sewer pits with no dimension. But they weren't the eyes of a killer. They were more like lost, little, boy eyes renting space in the head of a man. Not a good sign. He could be less predictable than most assholes and more dangerous.

"I need to kill you quickly, or lose my future."

"It's about money."

He flinched.

"Honor?"

"A bit of both, but the truth of the matter is that it doesn't matter why I kill you, only that I do." The cold hollowness of his voice resonated inside her. It didn't scare Sadie. It made her friggin mad.

A young waiter in a cowboy hat arrived at their table with a tray full of steaks, salad and beer. Shifting her gaze she took in the young man: twenties, handsome in a country-singer kind of way.

"I ordered for us," Leon said.

"You assumed I would eat with you?"

The young cowboy looked from Leon to Sadie, shrugged and put a plate of food and drinks down in front of each of them.

When the cowboy finished setting down their food and moved out of hearing range, Leon said, "I wanted us to look normal."

"A woman and her assassin, normal?" Sadie narrowed her eyes.

"I want to make a deal with you. I have already taken the first step to show you I mean well." He passed her his cell phone, which showed a photo of a man handing a vial to the receptionist at the Brownstone Vet Clinic. "Your dog will survive."

Sadie's heart burst with joy. She gave him a solid nod. This had to be the strangest negotiation in history.

"So you see I kept my end of a bargain. I promised you the antidote for poison if you showed up. You showed up and I delivered. I keep my word." The light reflecting off the sparks of orange in his eyes made him look like a hungry animal. "Now I want to offer you a deal."

"What do you have in mind?"

"I am doing this for the KOTL."

Sadie nodded.

"They. . ."

"Yes, I know. They protect the Emerald Tablets." What a pile of hoo-haw with relish.

Leon tilted his head and screwed up his mouth. "Something like that. Look I don't understand it all."

"But you want to make me a deal on their behalf. I get that. What can I offer you?"

"They want you dead, because you're a threat."

She nodded and waited.

"You must have some information I could take to them. I wouldn't have to kill you if you gave it to me."

"Hmm. I could just kill you." The words slipped right out of Sadie's mouth. They weren't the best ones for a negotiation. Going for the jugular was not always wise. But Sadie had never been one to want to talk things over. She liked action.

A sly-smile slid across his face. "You could. But

we both know they would send another assassin and another until you're dead." He left his point hanging in the air like a well-poised dagger.

Sadie yawned. "This game is getting tiresome."

The guitar player started another song. This one was louder and harder to ignore. Something about long-legged Betty.

"Do we have a deal then?"

"Possibly." She leaned back and folded her arms in front of her. "First, tell me exactly what information you're looking for."

He winced.

She waited.

"Hell, if I know."

Sadie lifted a brow

"I assumed you would know what it is."

"Nope."

His eyes darkened to a deathly shade of cold, like death itself. He raised his napkin to his mouth, dabbed it, then put it down. With his other hand he reached for hers.

Odd, that he would want to connect with her, but

maybe he needed that physical connection to seal the deal. Sadie left her hand on the table, allowing his hairy hand to cover it. His skin felt clammy at first and then she felt a sharp prick.

"Ouch." She pulled her hand back. A single drop of blood dribbled on top of her skin. She rubbed at it. Looking up she saw his smile widen.

Her body started trembling. Her head felt heavy as if a toxic mixture of tar had been poured into it and the dark mass trickled into every corner of her mind and then her body. The room spun. Painful spasms gripped her stomach. What had he given her? She stood up to make an escape. Her legs shook and she couldn't get her balance. She tried to scream, but she had no voice. Her legs gave way and she collapsed to the floor.

The spinning room turned black.

***

Sebastian couldn't believe Sadie left him naked, chained to her bed. He pulled and pulled on the handcuffs, until his arms hurt like hell. He took a breath and kept pulling until his wrists bled and the pain reached a level that calmed his mind.

He grunted. *Sadie would pay for this.* He shook his wrists. Made of steel, the cuffs weren't breakable and the fucking bed poles were just as strong. He was stuck. *Godverdomme.*

The handcuff keys sat on the bedside table within his reach, if he had free arms. His cell phone lay tucked in the pocket of his jeans, which were on the floor, also out of reach. Should he scream for help? The windows and door were closed and locked. No one would hear him.

Fucked. He had to face it. He was fucked.

The room still smelled of Sadie's strawberry shampoo, which only made his predicament worse. He groaned. "All is fair in love and doggy-whatever," be damned. Pulling on the cuffs again, he called out in pain.

What the hell was Sadie up to? He pulled again on his cuffs and the pain in his wrists increased. Probably meeting someone... He paused on that thought. Probably meeting the idiot who poisoned Cassy. And tried to kill her. He growled.

She wouldn't. She wouldn't be so crazy as to meet with the assassin. He groaned again.

He had grown closer to Sadie than to anyone else in the world. That was what he'd been trying to tell her. When he held her in his arms and her heart beat against his, he felt like they were one. It didn't matter how silly that sounded. It's what he felt. As if they had become connected, heart, mind and soul.

And that mind connection could really suck. Sadie had gone out on her own mission to capture the assassin. Alone.

He had to get out of there. Had to go to her. Get her out of danger. He pulled again on the cuffs and cried out in pain. Sweat poured from his skin. How could he protect her?

Closing his eyes he focused on escape. There had to be a way. In his mind he created the image of how he would do it. There had to be a way.

He took a deep breath and silently counted: *een, twee, drie*. When he hit *drie*, with all his energy he pulled on the headboard, and at the same time swung his legs up and over like a gymnast. His weight tipped the bed thirty degrees before it fell back into place. Maybe he could make his plan work. He tried again, and made it to forty five degrees. The third time he made it to fifty five degrees and the bed hovered vertical in the air for a couple of seconds, before it flipped onto its side and his feet hit the ground. Success.

He grunted. If they were going to stay together, Sadie would have to learn to behave. There had to be ground rules in a partnership. Like you don't leave your lover butt-naked, chained to the bed. Especially when danger neared. *Godverdomme.*

What next Houdini?

There was no way he could make it through the door with the bed on his back. For that matter, there was no way he could unlock the door without hands. He stepped to his jeans, sweat pouring off him and dripping onto the floor. He stood on one leg of his pants with one foot and with the toes of the other nudged the cell phone out of the back pocket. His shoulders ached from the strain of carrying the bed, but he focused on his mission. After several minutes, he freed the cell phone.

A gleeful moment of triumph flew through his body for a whole seconds and then stopped.

How the hell could he use the phone? Big men have big toes and he had little dexterity in them. He pointed his big toe as if he were a gorilla attempting to dance a ballet and tried to hit the keys. The funny tone that came from the mobile indicated he had succeeded in hitting several numbers at once.

His red-head had pulled one over on him this time. Double-O-Red, that's what he called her when he was angry. He'd make her pay. Oh yeah, big time. He smiled at that thought and let his body rest for a minute.

He tried pointing his toe again, and tapping the damn thing. Again his efforts resulted in a clamor of different tones. He tried again. And again. And again. With his luck he'd activate the 911 line and have to explain to them his situation. Heat rose to his face at the thought. He groaned. How could he have let this happen?

Oh yeah. He hadn't been thinking with his brain. He clenched his jaw.

Seb looked at the phone again, a wonderful modern invention, but no use to him at that moment.

He exhaled. No point in being a wimp. The phone was his best chance to get out. He tried again. And again. And then he heard a voice.

"Hello," Seb called out. "Hello, can you hear me?"

"Buddy, you don't sound good." It was Xander, his best friend.

"I'm butt naked, and chained to a bed."

Xander snickered. "Sadie?"

"Sadie."

"You two have all the fun." Xander laughed harder.

"She's in trouble. I know it. I feel it. I've got to get to her."

Xander stopped laughing. "Tell me where you are. I'll get you help."

"Sadie's place."

"Done." Xander clicked off.

Now Sebastian had to wait. Wait and wonder what fucked-up mess she'd gotten herself into this time. There had to be ground rules. He'd sensed she was up to something. He should have asked her more questions before they made out. *Oh yeah, Sherlock, as if that would have been possible. As soon as she touched your body you were lost.*

A tingly feeling in his gut yelled at him. Sadie was in danger. He just knew it.

Godverdomme, he sucked at waiting. Seconds passed like hours. Sweat pouring from his body pooled on the hardwood floor.

Sadie. . .

CHAPTER TWELVE

Even if he got free, Seb had no fucking

idea where to look for Sadie.

Well that wasn't quite true. After he lost her in
Amsterdam, and then again in Egypt, he'd hatched a
back-up plan. A man needed to be resourceful to stay
with a woman like Sadie. Her company cell phone, the
one she used to contact the CIA assholes had an extra
chip in it she didn't know about. Luckily the CIA techies
hadn't sniffed it out yet. It hadn't been easy to steal and
tamper with it, but he'd done it. There was more than
one devious player in their relationship.

Sebastian's friend Seamus who worked for
Interpol and understood all the spy-geeky stuff, assured
him it was the latest technology and virtually

impossible to detect with regular sensors. Apparently, you had to know what you were looking for to find it. Anyway, it was on her cell and if he activated an app on his phone, he could find her.

His gut twisted. The weight of the bed on his back, and the strain on his shoulders from the uncomfortable position they were forced into, were nothing compared to the frustration of not being able to locate Sadie.

The two New York City policemen who came to his rescue didn't laugh. They didn't even ask him a lot of questions. They looked him up and then down and shrugged.

"The keys are on the bedside table." Seb said.

The older one nodded and scooped them up in his hand. It took a minute to release him from the bed.

Sebastian thanked them, and the cops left. He heard the younger one say to his partner, "Hope she was worth it."

After Seb pulled on his pants he checked his cell. According to the tracking app linking him to Sadie, she was in Times Square. He took the Beretta he kept in

New York from the cupboard, shoved it into the back of his pants, grabbed his jacket and started running.

Ten minutes later, as he neared his destination, the signal started moving. *Great, a moving target.* He wiped his brow and looked around. He found himself in front of a cowboy steak joint. In New York? Why not? The red dot on his phone indicated Sadie was coming towards him.

See, Seb, life always turns around, if you give it time. He smirked. *Unless you run out of time.* Sadie where the hell are you?

A jingle from his phone alerted him to a text coming in. Could it be Sadie? He checked. ID: Brownstone Vet Clinic. He opened it. "The vial with the antidote was received and we gave it to Cassy as per the instructions. He's already looking better. I'll update you on the hour. Dr.Shned."

So Sadie had succeeding in getting Casanova the medicine he needed. But at what cost? She loved that dog enough to risk anything. The flashing red light on the locating app moved closer.

Out of the door to Jimmy's Steakhouse emerged

a man carrying an unconscious woman. Sadie. A waiter ran around him and lifted his hand in the air to hail a cab.

Seb didn't recognize the man holding his woman. Was she knocked out? Had he hurt her? Seb strode over to him. "I'll take her," he said, putting his arms forward and giving the guy a hard stare. The man looked older than him and soft. Seb could take him easily, if he had to.

The man's dark eyes stared back at him. "The lady has had too much to drink."

A yellow taxi pulled up and the waiter said, "Here you go, sir."

Pulling his eyes away from Seb, the man walked over to the cab. The waiter opened the back door. Carefully, the man with the dark eyes placed Sadie inside.

Seb pushed him aside and got in the back with her, lifting her head to place it on his lap.

Without a word, the man took the front, passenger seat. His confident demeanor grated on Seb's nerves, but he'd have to wait to punch him later. His first priority was Sadie. Seb gave the address of their apartment to the driver and softly moved tendrils of her red hair from her pale face.

The taxi accelerated away from the curb.

"What did you do to her?" Seb asked.

He shrugged. "She'll be awake soon."

"Why?"

The taxi turned left. Seb stared at the back of the driver's head. To get to their apartment they should have gone straight. Seb took a quick glance around the cab. It looked normal. "What the fuck?"

The strange man laughed, again. Damn. There was a raw meanness to that laugh, one Seb would never forget.

A thick wall of glass rose between the front and back seats. The door locks clicked into place. Seb held Sadie tighter. Never had he loved anyone more than her.

And now they were trapped.

CHAPTER THIRTEEN

Seb checked Sadie's pulse. Slow and steady.

He pulled his mobile out of his jacket pocket and turned it on, but there was no signal. None at all. The hair on the back of his neck rose. It should still be on, damn it. Pushing one button after another didn't help. *Godverdomme.* The car must have some sort of electronic blocker. *Who is this guy?*

Now what? If he figured out a way to open a door, he couldn't jump out with Sadie unconscious. He had to wait to see what the asshole did next. He looked around assessing the situation.

The car drove through town to the docks. A boat? They were going to a fucking boat?

They came to a stop beside a twenty seven foot

Kingfisher, a motor boat built for fishing. What the hell?

The driver, built like a Schwarzenegger wanna-be, opened the door. Pointing a Glock in Seb's face he said, "Get out. Bring the girl." His voice had a grisly sound to it.

Sebastian edged out first and then pulled Sadie out carefully. He kept his back to the men to shield her. As he held her in his arms, she winked at him. A hallelujah dance played through his nervous system. *If they could both fight, the odds of them winning more than doubled.* He turned to face the men and stared down at them. "What now?"

"Come aboard. I will fix you a drink. We will talk. And maybe we can come to some agreement."

"Agreement?"

"After the drone didn't kill your girlfriend, I did more research on her background. I found out all about you. You have money, Mr. Wilde."

So that was what he wanted. "Name your price."

"Come on board. We will talk. Man to man."

Sadie did a good job of looking out of it. That man-to-man comment would anger her, but she hid all emotion from her face. If they survived this, he'd have to tell her what a good actress she was. If...

With Sadie nestled in his arms, Sebastian followed the lead guy onto the boat and into the cabin. The driver with his gun followed behind. Sweat trickled down Seb's spine. But knowing it was about money, made him feel better. He could deal with greedy people. Just not deranged ones.

"My name is Leon Krykos the fourth. Put Sadie on the sofa." The orifice pointed to a bench with a cushion on it.

Seb lowered her carefully to the platform and pushed her hair out of her face. "She's so out of it."

"Your woman will be fine." He sat at a table and motioned for Seb to sit at the chair opposite him. "Before you sit down, give me your gun."

Seb handed over his Berretta and sat.

"I have orders to kill Sadie."

Seb stared at him feeling sweat slide down his face.

"I met with her, because I don't like murder and I thought I could make a deal. If she gave me the information the KOTL want, then I could let her go, but she says she doesn't know where the tablets are hidden and has no map or information to find them. She says she has nothing."

Seb nodded again. "So now you want money?"

"I don't want to kill her."

"Won't they come after you, if you don't?"

"I don't think I'm that important to them. I will be considered a failure. That's alright with me, as long as I have the money I need to live well and protect myself."

"I see. So you want to let us free."

"Not exactly. My failure will result in the loss of my inheritance. I expect you to match that amount, or there's no deal."

"And how much would that be?"

"Twenty million."

Seb didn't flinch. There was no way he could possibly raise that much money, but obviously this asshole didn't know that. "Twenty?"

"I know you don't have it on hand." He tilted his head as if he knew everything there was to know about everything. Arrogant. Asshole. Prick. "But they say you have the golden touch in the art business. I'm betting that over the next few years your accounts will grow nicely. I want a part of that." He turned his gaze to Sadie who looked comatose. "You can pay me a nice yearly dividend. Say five mill." A sly smile swept across his face, as wily as a fucking weasel. "The woman's worth it."

Seb stared at him.

"I know you keep a close watch on the looted art market. If your regular business can't bring in the money, it can. You can make our arrangement work."

Seb's gut wrenched. "If I agree to your deal, what assurance do I have you will stick to it."

"Check up on me. I don't kill people."

"But the KOTL?"

"Yes, well I can't control them. They may send more assassins. You will have to deal with them one at a time."

Seb leaned back against the cushion. "And if I don't pay?"

"That would be most unfortunate for both of

you." His *geiten neuker* smile returned. "I've hired five guards. It's my backup plan. They will keep you imprisoned, until the next KOTL, hit man arrives." Running a hand through his oily, black hair he paused for a minute. "Killing you will be as easy as shooting ducks in a pond for a pro."

Seb fantasized about reaching across the table and strangling him, but the man's thug held his gun steady, aimed at Seb's chest. Doing something stupid now, might feel good for a micro-second, but then he would be dead and Sadie. . .

"Well Mr. Wilde. I have made my offer clear. What do you say?"

Seb could feel Sadie's movement. He didn't dare look her way. That would draw attention to her. Instead he stood up. The thug went rigid with attention and his gun remained pointed at Seb's heart.

Leon kept eye contact with Seb and rose. "Don't do anything stupid, Mr. Wilde."

A Japanese-glass, fishing float flew through the air and knocked muscle man square on the forehead like a glass beach ball. "Don't call my man stupid."

Sadie's sweet voice sounded strong and clear.

***

Sadie had listened to every word the men spoke. Yada yada yada. . .Would the man from the KOTL ever get to the point? Sadie's head throbbed and her stomach churned as if a million deranged bees were holding a rave inside. Her fingers itched to move. Leon was going down. As soon as he finished spitting out his plan, she'd nail him. Were all Greek millionaires so long-winded? Sheesh. She listened, and listened, keeping her body as lifeless-looking as she could. Stealing a look around the cabin, she figured out where everyone stood and what she could use as a weapon.

Finally, Leon finished his side of the negotiation. What an arrogant ass.

In one swift movement Sadie rose, reached for the glass ball covered in fish net sitting on the table beside her and with all her strength threw it at the minion with the gun. Got him. Yes! Right between the eyes. Her years of pitching on the Seattle Sea Birds team had come in handy once again.

"Arrgh," cried out the guard as he stumbled back from the impact and put his hands to his head. Sebastian was on him with a flash.

Sadie jumped behind Leon and, before he could say a word, and she had him by the throat in a deadly choke-hold.

CHAPTER FOURTEEN

The elder Leonidas Krykos III did not

know how to explain to the KOTL leaders that his son
had failed to kill Sadie Stewart. He had been summoned
by the council, which meant they probably already
knew the details. All the same, he had to plead his son's
case.

They met in an ancient church, in Cairo. Would
they terminate him, or his son? It was possible. They
knew too much and had proved themselves useless.
Less than useless. Leon sighed. He had thought old age
would bring its rewards, but it seemed to bring nothing
but disappointments.

And where was his son?

Dropped off at the door, the older Leon waved to his driver and body-guard to carry on. This was one event he needed to attend alone, completely alone. He had sworn an oath to the KOTL and had failed them. Dressed in his best, black, business suit, he pulled his shoulders back and lifted his chin, determined to look undefeated to the end, while his insides shrank with defeat and his gut twisted with worry.

Inside the chamber five people sat at a long table. The smell of mold and sweat laced with anger hovered in the air. None of them stood, but they all stared at him through round holes in their dark green hoods. The center person, known as Asteria, lifted her arm and pointed to the chair opposite their table, indicating that Leon should sit there, alone in the center of the room.

Leon sat. His breathing labored as his throat constricted under the gaze of the council. He cleared his throat. "I'm sorry," he said. Two words he had vowed as a young man never to say. "My son failed. I have failed."

Silence. Deadly silence. The menacing eyes continued to spear his resolve.

"I thought with his knowledge of technology, he could eliminate Sadie Stewart, but. . ."

"She still lives." The voice, which came from Asteria, was low and menacing like a rogue wave ready to collapse on top of him.

"He built a highly sophisticated. . ."

"Drone. You thought you could take her out with a drone."

Leon nodded. "When the skilled assassin failed to kill her in Venice in a conventional way, I figured we had to try something different. It was my turn to find a solution, so I talked with him."

"You were thinking outside the box."

Leon nodded. The comment had not been meant as a compliment. The derision in Asteria's voice raked Leon's senses as surely as the razor sharp claws of a raptor. More like outside his own coffin.

"The woman must die," she said.

The four men on the panel began pounding the wooden table. "*Bang, bang, bang!*" The sound grew louder.

"I did what I thought best," said Leon with as much contriteness as he could muster. "If. . ."

The pounding continued.

Leon raised his voice to be heard over the noise.

"If you would give me one more chance."

Asteria lifted her right hand and the pounding stopped. The sudden silence hit him harder than the pounding. He tried to breathe, but his chest tightened to the point that little air got in. He firmed his jaw. "I will kill Sadie Stewart. I will find a way. I swear."

"Do you swear on your life?"

"Yes."

"On your son's life?"

Leon hesitated, which surprised him. Not until this moment had he realized how important little Leon was to him. After another second, he said, "Yes."

The room fell silent.

A shiver stole up Leon's spine. How on earth would he kill her? There had to be a way. There had to be someone he could buy that could get the job done. He was no soldier or assassin. And nor was his son. "I will find a way."

Asteria nodded. "Then Sadie Stewart will die."

CHAPTER FIFTEEN

Sebastian arrived back in Amsterdam too late to meet with Walter Easterbrook, the British dot-com guy who bought art for prestige. Walking home from Central Station he mused about how little that meeting mattered to him. So what if he missed the biggest art deal of his career. There would be others. There was only one Sadie Stewart.

When he opened his apartment door he found his best friend Xander sitting in his favorite chair, drinking his Belgian beer. The distinct aroma of baby powder hit him. His eyes dropped to the baby Mauritz, sound asleep in a carrier on the floor.

"Xander."

His friend raised a finger in the classic, just a second pose. The sounds of crowds cheering at a soccer match blared on Seb's big-screen TV mounted on the wall. Sebastian closed the door, dropped his bags and without a word headed to the fridge for a beer.

When he returned to the living area, Xander had migrated to the couch and Sebastian took the chair. "What's the score?"

"Two for Sadie. Zero for you."

"Fuck you."

"You gotta stop thinking with your dick."

He ran a hand through his hair. A hell of a homecoming. "Everything worked out."

"According to who? You're so fucked in the head, man. She left you naked, chained to a bed. I have the picture by the way, courtesy of New York's finest. Then you got kidnapped and almost killed."

"Almost. You have to remember the almost part."

"That's the third time you put your life at risk. You could play with less dangerous women."

"But no one is like Sadie."

"Is she worth it?"

"Hell yeah."

Xander threw a cushion at his head. And the Ajax team scored on the TV.

CHAPTER SIXTEEN

New York City

𝒮adie sat back in her folding chair in the

park soaking in the beauty of the day. She smiled at
Beatrice who studied the playing cards she held in her
hands as if they held the keys to the universe. Bee's
bridge friends had declined their invitation to get
together for a game of bridge, so it was just Beatrice
and herself this time. They were playing gin rummy and
Bee was cheating. Sadie was sure of it and out ten
bucks. No one could win that many games. Sadie
watched her closely, trying to catch her at it, but
cheating at gin didn't seem like a big deal after what
they had been through.

Cassy, dozing in the late afternoon heat lay on

the ground in such a way that his body touched both women. He'd gone on a five mile run with Sadie in the morning, and acted like his old frisky, puppy-self. Sadie's life seemed normal again, or at least as normal as her double-life could ever be.

Sadie reached down and scratched under his ear. The poisoning made her realize just how attached she'd become to the flea bitten pooch. Cassy rolled on his back and she scratched his tummy. His tail thumped. There was something perfect about their relationship, she had never imagined existed between a woman and a dog. The predictability, the unconditional love, the furry wonder of it all.

"Gin." Bee smiled her winner's smile as she slammed her cards down on the table. What the hell did she do this time?

Sadie nodded and put her cards down. She had come close this time, but hadn't made it.

Beatrice took all the cards and shuffled them with the dexterity of a Vegas dealer. No doubt she'd learned her cheating skills in the back rooms of the casinos. While she waited for her cards, Sadie did a glance-around to check the park out. Everything seemed safe. *For now.*

Bee started dealing. "So where's the Dutch giant?"

"Amsterdam. But he'll be back tomorrow."

"He's quite the catch."

Sadie laughed. "I'm not sure who's catching who, but I get what you mean. He's okay." She winked at Bee.

"That good, heh?"

"Oh yeah." Ripples of pleasure ran along Sadie's skin short-circuiting her thoughts as she remembered their last night together. She hoped she wasn't blushing, but she probably was.

"So why don't you quit your modeling-or-whatever job you do and be with him. Life's short honey."

"I like what I do."

"Uh huh. Is it, you can't give up the free lipstick, or you can't give up getting shot at?"

Sadie bit her bottom lip. "Maybe both."

Beatrice picked up her cards and shook her head. "Sooner or later he'll get tired of waiting for you."

"He's not exactly waiting. We're together lots."

Bee shrugged. "But it could be so much more."

Possibly. Sadie didn't like to think about that. It was too big, too. . . well big. Thinking of commitment to a man made her skin crawl and her feet itchy. She'd been married once and that had been the biggest mistake of her life. Another marriage could screw things up. She liked her life the way it was "My boss would have a heart attack."

"Fuck the boss. You only live once, honey. There are no dress rehearsals on this runway. Go for it."

"And this comes from a lady who likes living alone."

"I never met the right guy. But you and Sebastian..." Bee put her cards face down on the table. "That's a once-in-a-lifetime thing. Don't be stupid."

"Hmmm. I like my independence."

Beatrice raised her shut-up hand. Her new finger-nail polish Sadie bought her, called Color me Bad, glistened in the sunlight. "You like it too much for your own good. I tell ya, he won't wait around forever. And there are plenty of other women who would like him in their bed."

Bed. Just the thought of being with Sebastian in bed warmed her body. "He says he likes my independent spirit."

"Uh-huh. Is that before or after you get it on?"

Definitely before. Maybe Beatrice had a point. Maybe it was time to let go a little and share her life more fully with Sebastian. Sweet Jesus, he'd proved himself worthy over and over again.

Bee studied Sadie's face as if she could read her thoughts. "Tell me what you like about him."

Sadie exhaled. "He's the most honest, straight forward person I've ever met. He says what he means, and does what he says he's going to do. He's a good solid man."

"Integrity—Check." She winked at her. "Doesn't exactly warm my blood, but I get it."

"He cares about other people. Not in a false way, but in a get out there and fight for them way."

"What do you mean? Like charity work?"

"He gives lots of money to charities, but it's more than that. He investigates leads about looted art, because he wants to fix the wrongs that have been done. He wants to give back to the victims, people he doesn't even know. He believes in justice."

"A warrior. That's sexy, but you're still not painting him hot."

"Oh, I didn't think I needed to do that. Just look at him. He's six feet five inches of hard muscled, alpha male."

"That's more like it."

Sadie laughed. "Are you looking for dirty details Miss. Beatrice?"

"Can you blame me?" Her lined face lit up with a smile.

"Yeah, he's awesome in bed. But I'm not going there. That's between us."

"Okay, so we got a handsome hero, oozing with testosterone... who has integrity and knows his way around your body. I agree that's nice. Very nice. But not enough to get married."

"But there's more, so much more."

"Spit it out."

"It's the way he makes me feel."

"I thought you didn't want to talk about the sex."

"Not the sex, at least, not just the sex. When I'm with him he makes me feel totally loved and honored. Like I'm the most important person in his world. I can tell him anything. It's like he's my best friend, as well as my lover."

Beatrice moved her arms, pretending to play an invisible violin. "Like he completes you?"

"You asked." Sadie could feel heat dance across her cheeks. She hadn't verbalized her feelings before. It had been easier to keep her emotions close to her heart where no one could make fun of them or use them to hurt her. She'd learned long ago that the world crushes those who expose themselves. She folded her arms in front of her. "Words just make my feelings sound silly.

"Like a love song." Beatrice stopped playing her imaginary instrument. "Shake your cheekbones Sadie. You are head over red stilettoes in love. Denying it will only cause you and Sebastian heart ache. It's time to accept your feelings and act on them.

"I'll think about it." She tried to make a solemn face. "I'm just so used to going it alone, and then there's the whole issue we have about my job."

"A smart woman like you should be able to figure out how to make it work." Beatrice looked over her reading glasses. "When did you say Sebastian was returning?"

"Tonight."

***

Sadie dunked her head beneath a foot of rose scented bubbles in the bath tub, before she pulled out her work phone. She pushed the speed-dial number for Jeremiah Cole's office.

"Hi sugar, how are you doing?" His southern drawl set her at ease, as she knew he intended it to. Everything about Cole was calculated.

"Just wanted to tell you that I've completed my report and sent it in. I went over it several times. I think every detail is in there." Of course he would know that, so why was she bothering to tell him?

"And?"

"Did you find out more on the KOTL?"

"No. We have questioned Leon Krykos IV for hours. I don't think he knows anything."

"What will you do with him?"

"We're playing a waiting game. He sits in a comfortable, albeit not luxurious, room on foreign soil, not knowing what will happen to him next, not even knowing who is holding him. He only knows that we act on your behalf. Detaining him could make him tell us more. His father is going crazy looking for him. We may be able to make a deal with him. We're letting both of them sweat for now. And as for their organization, the KOTL, I'm hoping they will figure out it's not in their best interest to keep harassing you. We'll see."

"I've been reading my great-aunt's journal."

"Anything new?" Anxiety laced his words. What did he know about Aunt Emma that he wasn't sharing? Sadie scrunched her face. Was he being sketchy or was it her imagination? One could get too paranoid in the shadow world.

"Not yet," she replied.

"Would you tell me if you did find something?"

She laughed. "Maybe. Look I've got to go. Things to do."

"Sebastian's coming tonight?"

He knew. Of course he knew. "Yup."

"I've said it before and I'll say it again. You need to lose him, honey. One day he'll get you killed. Or he'll get killed by getting in the way."

"So far, he's saved my ass twice. I think I'll keep him."

"Your feelings run too deep. He matters too much. And someone, someday, will use that love to get to you. I don't like busting your love-bubble, but I care about you, Sadie. I don't want to see you hurt. Or dead. You need to end your relationship."

Sadie sank her head beneath the bubbles and felt the warmth of the water soak into her skin. Like hell, Cole, like hell. When she re-emerged, he had stopped nagging.

"Cole, you don't get to tell me what to do in my personal life."

But the line was dead. He'd already gone. She threw her cell against the wall. Logic told her the friggin master spy was right. Love told her a whole other story.

After an hour in the bath Sadie, wrapped herself from head to foot in towels and then lay back on her sofa. She had a couple hours to spare before she would get ready for Sebastian. Enough time to read more of her great-aunt's journal. Touching the soft-leather, book jacket, she stopped for a moment and tried to imagine the woman talking directly to her. A voice from the past.

Emma-Mae wrote, "I didn't want to put my lover in danger."

CHAPTER SEVENTEEN

Sebastian arrived two hours later. She couldn't wait to tell him what she had learned from her aunt's diary, but Sebastian had his own surprise.

He dropped to one knee before her.

Oh no. This can't be happening. I can't let it happen. Not marriage. That's way too much commitment. Not marriage. No. Not again. I can't be a wife. It's not for me. Been there, done that; have the scars and a shredded tee shirt. Cole would kill me.

Sebastian's blue eyes, the color of the sky at dawn, held hers with all the love he held for her in his big, earnest heart. How could she possibly say no to the best man she had ever known.

A small smile slid across his face.

She couldn't do this. A marriage of two globe-trotting, independent people would be a disaster. They couldn't manage to keep a dog safe. How could they expect to keep themselves safe? It couldn't work.

He cocked a brow as if he heard her thoughts.

Despite all the reasons she shouldn't consider a proposal, the moment swept her away like a fairy tale. Some tough spy! Her heart raced. Her love for him was the truest love she had ever known, greater than she thought humanly possible. And he had dropped to his knee for her. "Sebastian," she said, reaching for his face. She traced it with her hand. "We need to talk."

"It's my turn to talk," he said in his low husky voice. He pulled a small, royal blue velvet pouch from his back pocket. "Sadie."

The way he said her name undid her. *Oh my goodness.* She didn't deserve him. She swiped at the tears flowing down her cheeks. When had she started crying? The whole situation was beyond, way beyond, anything she had ever fantasized about. "Just give me the ring."

He laughed. "No."

She sniffed. Where were the tissues when you needed one? Her mascara was probably running, and her eyes would get all puffy and ugly red. And her heart beat so loud she was sure it would burst. Wasn't a woman supposed to be poised at this life-turning moment? She swiped at another tear.

"I have loved you since the moment I met you."

Cliché. I can deal with clichés. Forcing herself to breathe deeper, she sniffed again.

"You are the most beautiful woman in the world."

Like she hadn't heard that before. But coming from him, it meant so much more.

"I'm not talking about your hot body, or your dedication to justice.

She laughed. Couldn't help it. What man talks about justice when he proposes to his love? Only Sebastian. A one of a kind. Her one of a kind.

He laughed with her. "Seriously, I love how you care about everyone and how you put your life on the line to make the world a safer place."

"Does that mean you accept me being a spy?"

The words spilled out of her. If he couldn't accept her for herself, this would never work.

His eyes darkened. "Sadie, in a perfect world you would not have to be a spy. I understand why you do it, and I respect you for it."

"But?"

"I long for the day when you will let others carry on the fight and settle into being with me and have a family."

A family? She gulped, imagining a little Sadie chasing a little Sebastian around her legs with a bottle of pink nail polish gripped in her hand. She gulped again. And then there was JaJa, her adopted son. He could have a real family. The image was nice, but... "Sebastian, I'm not ready for that."

"I know." He slid the ring from the pouch. It was perfect, a white gold band with a ruby at its center surrounded by sparkling diamonds. Sadie swallowed. It truly was a fitting symbol of their love.

"All I ask is that you commit to me, to us, now and forever. The rest, I have faith, will happen."

"Sebastian I love you more than I can say. I love

everything about you, but mostly I love that when we are together I feel whole and happy and complete. The only promise I can make is that I will love you and only you forever."

"Good enough for me." He stood up and slipped the ring on her finger. It glistened in the morning sunlight.

"Oh Sebastian." Her heart burst with happiness, into millions of kaleidoscopic shards of pure joy. Never had she felt so wild, so free, so filled with love.

"It was my great-grandmothers, fashioned in Amsterdam." Sebastian's voice gentled. "This is forever Sadie. You and me, forever. I don't want any of the hip new-monogamy stuff where we move on to others when the mood catches us. Just you. Just me. Together, forever."

"It's perfect." Stretching out her hand she stared at his offering of love, a symbol she would proudly wear for the rest of her life. "So perfect."

Sebastian looked down at her. "Is my kick-ass spy crying?"

"You tell anyone, and I will kick your ass."

He laughed and with his giant fingers wiped away her tears with the gentleness of a whisper. They stayed like that for a minute. Her looking at the ring. He stroking her face. A frozen moment in time.

Balance? The word she had thought so much about for the last six months sprang into the forefront of her mind. What happened to her dream of finding balance in her double life? *Oh hell. Balance sucks. It lacks excitement. It lacks reality. Forget balance. I will live my life fully—push all the limits. With Sebastian at my side.* The tears stopped.

Sadie looked up and gave him a seductive smile. She lifted a brow. "What now?"

"Payback time." His voice went low and ragged to the point of scary as he gave her his killer smile. The one that sent tingles to her lower belly.

Normally he'd have pulled her into his arms by now. But he hadn't. Nothing about this day was normal. What was he up to?

Out of his jacket pocket, he pulled two, red silk scarves and held them up, one in each hand. "What do they say? 'All is fair in love and... sex.'"

This is Not the End

Coming Soon

Till Danger Do Us Part

Mata Hari #5, a full length novel

Dear Readers,

Thanks for reading *Lovin' Danger*. I hope you enjoyed Sadie, her friends and the world I've created for them.

If you liked this book, the very best thing you can do is leave a review for it. Amazon.com is where I sell the majority of my books, but I would be thrilled to see reviews everywhere.

You can learn about me from my website:

http://jo-anncarson.com

Again, thank you...

my best,

Jo-Ann Carson

Smart, Sexy Suspense

Acknowledgements

My heartfelt thanks go to:

My husband, Piet, and daughters who are always there for me.

Dr. Philip Newey, my copy-editor, who straightens out my grammar.

Nina French, my cover designer extraordinaire, who knocked it out of the park again with her cover design.

Marisa Radcliffe my awesome beta-reader who catches all sorts of interesting things.

New York Times best-selling author, Mimi Barbour, for reading my arc and giving me an endorsement. As anyone who knows her can attest, her generosity of spirit knows no bounds.

And last, but never least, my writing buddies who support and inspire me.

The Mata Hari Series

#1 - Covert Danger

#2 - Born of Magic

#3 - Ancient Danger

Let me tell you about the other stories in the series.

Covert Danger

A single woman — A double life

High fashion model, Sadie Stewart, is a dedicated undercover CIA agent used to getting her man. But this time she's chasing a power-hungry international arms dealer stealing ancient Egyptian amulets. Brilliant, ruthless and slightly wacko, he's a hard catch. She's willing to risk everything to stop him, but the handsome Sebastian Wilde, who looks like a modern Viking, keeps getting in her way. Her independence is shaken as he stirs feelings in her that she thought only existed in fairy tales. Can she put their attraction aside and get the job done?

When Sebastian sees Sadie in a high-speed motor-boat flying down the Grand Canal in Venice, with the Italian military police hot on her tail, her beauty and courage intrigue him. He has a personal vendetta to stop the trading of looted art, and when it looks as though she's involved in that shady world, he decides to stop her. Could the femme fatale really be that evil?

Their adventure spans the globe, with scenes in Venice, Florence, Amsterdam, Cairo and New York.

Can they work together and stop the heist planned for the Met Museum of Art? Protecting the relics becomes their shared goal, but it's not all about ancient magic and power. Love hangs in the balance.

Born of Magic

A short story linking the first and second novels in the series.

The Egyptian Sorceress wants a child of her own. The arms-dealer wants power at any cost. Their desires conceive a son destined to change the world.

***

Ancient Danger

A single woman – a complicated life

International, super-model Sadie Stewart meets her Dutch lover Sebastian Wilde in Venice to celebrate their six month anniversary in style. But having lived a double life as a CIA operative for ten years, her life is never simple.

During a charity costume ball in an ancient Venetian palace, an assassin tries to take her out. Sebastian gets over-protective, which drives her crazy. Her old boss offers her information, but wants something in return.

Arms-dealer, Bakari al-Sharif is planning to steal more ancient Egyptian treasure. This time he's after a scarab from the tomb of Tutankhamen about to be revealed at Highclere Castle near London. Sadie is the only person who has ever gotten close to al-Sharif and lived. The CIA wants her to stop him.

Or at least that's what they say. When it comes to the world of espionage, the true motivation of the players is never clear.

Can Sadie return to the life of a spook and maintain a relationship with Sebastian? Can she nail the arms-dealer? Can she figure out why the masked man tried to kill her?

Life is complicated for Sadie Stewart.